Father Guards the Sheep

Iowa Short Fiction Award

Father Guards the Sheep

Sari Rosenblatt

University of Iowa Press, Iowa City

University of Iowa Press, Iowa City 52242
Copyright © 2020 by Sari Rosenblatt
www.uipress.uiowa.edu
Printed in the United States of America
Text design by Sara T. Sauers

Printed on acid-free paper

Library of Congress Cataloging-in-Publication Data
Names: Rosenblatt, Sari, author.
Title: Father Guards the Sheep / Sari Rosenblatt.
Description: Iowa City: University of Iowa Press, [2020] |
    Series: Iowa Short Fiction Award
Identifiers: LCCN 2020006591 (print) |
    LCCN 2020006592 (ebook) |
    ISBN 9781609387440 (paperback; acid-free paper) |
    ISBN 9781609387457 (ebook)
Classification: LCC PS3618.O83375 A6 2020 (print) |
    LCC PS3618.O83375 (ebook) |
    DDC 813/.6—dc23
LC record available at https://lccn.loc.gov/2020006591
LC ebook record available at https://lccn.loc.gov/2020006592

To Nora and Anne

Schlaf, Kindlein, Schlaf

"Sleep baby sleep

The father guards the sheep

The mother shakes the little trees

There falls a little dream"

—GERMAN LULLABY

Contents

Father Guards the Sheep

Daughter of Retail

RETAIL WORKS LIKE THIS: Someone walks in the door and she's yours. You may not fall in love, but you have to put her body before yours. You must see whatever it is she wants to show you; smell her smell; satisfy her. You must sell yourself before you sell the suit.

I was twelve when I started working in my father's store—*Schmurr's: Say what you need; get what you want. We got the whole Schmurr.*

"Shorten the slogan, Irv, for Christ's sake," complained the eighty-year-old accountant.

"Shorten your mouth and maybe you'll learn to add," said my father, circling a number a half-mile down from the top of the ledger. They sat in Schmurr's glass-encased office, which gave my father a commanding view of who was selling or talking or stealing. The accountant's white hair had one large bald spot, a pink planet of a spot whose topography was speckled with mauve and brown gasses. My father banged his index finger into the ledger as though hammering a nail into oak. "To the moon, Alice!" my father yelled at the little old man, betraying his equal disdain for women and math morons.

In his own bald head, my father could figure columns of numbers the length of Rubber Avenue. Though he was a merchant of wearable goods—anything that could be hung on a rack or stacked on a shelf—what he loved most was numbers. He'd sell them if he could. But he couldn't. Schmurr's New York Bargain Goods was his inheritance, his own father's most successful enterprise (after the Naugatuck screw factory went belly up), and it was his duty as oldest son to take it over. Numbers would have to wait or he could do them on the side. Just as a fine artist must sometimes steal time to do his art, my father had to steal time to figure his columns. You could say he stole time from his children, but he wouldn't have known what to do with us, anyway.

Every night he'd bring home stacks of hard-bound, blue books and as we watched Walter Cronkite or *What's My Line?* he would add and figure, mostly in an effort to catch the accountant in a mistake. I sat on the couch parallel to his and we parallel-watched Peggy Cass and Kitty Carlisle try to determine if someone was deceitful or really a horse buckler from Idaho. My father kept his head down and followed columns from top to bottom. His pencil was a baton, going down, softening the sound of the loud horns. He was in a swoon over his numbers. Water pooled in his mouth but he was in too much of a reverie to swallow. He figured out loud, saying the numbers softly to himself like a man in prayer, raising his voice only when he found a mistake: "224,289,486,552,594,604, son of a bitch!"

This was what my father lived for. The rest of it—the store, the goods, the coats, the pants, the hats, the wife—was filler.

I was filler. Stuart, however, was something more. To my father, Stuart was a successfully computed multi-figure, multi-decimal, quarter-mile column. He was the captain of the Naugy High football team and the president of the Naugy High band. With shoulders as big as boulders, he could both command the marching band and plow into a fierce defensive line. The only bad thing about him was that people used his football prowess as a launching pad to diminish me. Seemingly respectable, law-abiding customers would come into our store and start striking me down with hammers, axes, small talk.

"You athletic like your brother? You fast on the field, quick with the ball, comfortable on the court?"

I could only look down at the linoleum, or out at the sky, clutch my bony clavicle and sigh, "Not really."

The truth was I was afraid to challenge myself physically because I knew I'd always fall short of Stuart. I didn't want to be short and I didn't want to find out if I was short. I'd wait to find out; I'd wait as long as I had to. In the meantime, I had to be something.

So when retail beckoned, when one evening making dinner my mother stuffed a hard-boiled egg into a raw, wet meatloaf and said, "Hon, you want to work at the store?" I clutched my clavicle, that thin, protective guardrail, and said, "All right." I saw retail as my only chance to be recognized as a rightful heir, to be considered an important, viable Schmurr.

Yet at twelve, I was only toying with my inheritance. Retail worried me. At its heart, retail is the art of getting familiar fast; of staring at a body you've never seen and summing up the size of its whole or its parts—either the whole oven roaster or, separately, her legs, thighs, breasts, back. Often in the course of doing business, you had to touch people. You had to zip, adjust, pull, snap, smooth, measure. If I was going to judge a woman's size, I needed more evidence. If I was going to touch her, I wanted a longer courtship.

I started by dusting purses. I showed great promise, so my mother began grooming me for bras. There was no soft coddling or slow cooking where retail was concerned. At Schmurr's my mother was all business: Schmurr's wife. Mrs. Schmurr's Department Store. And once I crossed the threshold of Schmurr's as a worker, I became—in the eyes of the public and probably of God—Schmurr's Daughter. The Daughter of Schmurr. There was no turning back. I could only stand and take my instruction. "If anyone asks about a bra," my mother told me, "you say, 'Playtex Cross Your Heart has good lift and separation.' If anyone asks about a girdle you say, 'Playtex Double Diamond has good tummy control.' Then come get me."

Waiting for my time to come, I hid in purses. The purse department was in the front of the store, yet it was hidden in the far wall of a tiny, three-sided alcove. The purses were right next to Schmurr's large display window and therefore were heated from the afternoon sun. The sun passed through the family of mannequins, passed the fake fall leaves taped to the window, and always found its way to me. The sun blessed and covered me and I became a baby beneath a receiving blanket. If I didn't fight it, I would have fallen asleep in the sunny tunnel of light and dust that shone down on purses.

Purses occupied the two top shelves of the alcove, and the other two shelves were stacked with diaper sets, baby blankets, baby boxed outfits, and baby boxed bath wear. Flanking the rows of shelving were racks of hanging baby clothes—rompers, overalls, acrylic pants with snap tops. Most of our customers—rubber workers who worked the assembly line across the street—didn't want purses. Only occasionally did they buy baby clothes. They needed the raw essentials—underwear, workpants, support hose. Still, purses were a great place to duck and cover, so I stayed there and did whatever I could to make the purses present themselves well.

There were vinyl purses with plastic handles, snaps, and single or double straps. There were vinyl clutches and vinyl shoulder bags with an array of different surfaces: rough, smooth, patched, pebbled, or alligator-look. There were some evening bags: beaded, lame, or dyeable. I arranged them by size and texture and color. Beyond that, they needed constant dusting since they were at the front of the store and seemed to catch all the dust and chemical residue spewed by our next-door neighbor, U.S. Rubber. I'd spray Windex again and again on the vinyl bags, wipe them clean, wipe them until they sparkled and shimmered and until the customers had thinned out and it was safe to leave. I tried to make purses my life's work. I tried to look busy and uninterruptable. I hoped nobody would find me. They always did.

"Little Girl!" they'd scream, as they ran in for their fifteen-minute break. "Blouses for big women! Stockings for big legs!" The questions got progressively harder and from time to time I'd have to leave my small alcove to stand in the aisle and field the assaults. "Little Girl! Blouses for big women with big busts!" "Little Girl! Stockings for fat legs and big butts!" I'd show them, tell them, then slip back to purses.

Stuart got to avoid retail for the fall season. He had football practice and was therefore excused until after Thanksgiving. When he helped at Schmurr's, winters and summers, he didn't have to do any dirty work, either. In Men's, where he was stationed, it was easier. Men came in and asked for things but they always seemed to acquiesce to whatever we had, to make decisions quickly, to buy it before they'd tried it on, to wear it even if it didn't fit. Women needed more time and pretty much always wanted to try on things. They wanted someone to counsel them or at least offer an opinion or a blessing. It was as if they were saying, "Pray for me. Please, pray for me."

Before I started working at the store, I too would be home for the fall season and for all the seasons. Most days after school, I would come home and lie on my bed, on the pink spread that always caught the afternoon light. I could have taught my dog, our old terrier, a thing or two about lying in patches of sun. I knew how to catch the sun and make it stay on me, how to let it warm my head, neck, the small of my back.

Stuart, three years older, was supposed to babysit me. He'd bring his football friends home after practice, around four thirty, before my parents got home from the store, and our kitchen table would be surrounded by a large sample of Naugy High Greyhounds eating two or three packages of Lorna Doones. My own room was right next door to the kitchen, in the former den, and even though Stuart would sometimes close the sliding pocket door that divided the two rooms I could clearly hear them. From my patch of sun, I could almost imagine I was sleeping. But I didn't imagine what they said. They spoke about Sky Bar tongues, Snow Ball breasts, Sugar Daddy legs. They talked of Almond Joys, Mounds, Milky Ways, and Spearmint Leaves. They were breast and thigh guys rushing Candy Land. Stuart didn't contribute much to the conversation except to laugh or say, "Shhh . . ." When they left, Stuart would open the pocket door that divided them from me and say, "Are you there?"

"No."

"Okay."

But it wasn't okay. I didn't want to hear it and I didn't want to see it and I wanted to stay in purses forever. I was in purses the day Verna Pixley rushed the main door of Schmurr's. I swear I heard glass spraying, as though she had crashed through the main display window, maiming the mannequins and wielding a semiautomatic rifle.

"Somebody quick!" she yelled to everyone. "I need a bra!"

I turned my back as soon as I could, squirted yet more Windex on a vinyl bag, and hoped one of the other salesgirls—Lena, Rita, Esther, Martha, Theresa—would come over and save me. I was not ready for this. It was too fast for me. I was not precocious in bras.

I made some fake, useless motions around the purses—touching the handles and fingering the clasps—hoping to look legitimately occupied, but she found me. "Little Girl! Fast, fast! I need a bra! Do you work here?" I turned around to face her, knowing as I did so that I had just left purses—probably, forever.

"Yes?" I said.

Walking out of the alcove, I stood in front of her and looked into her eyes, which were big and black and seemed to regard me with absolute shock, as if I was either her tormentor or savior.

"Can you help me?" she asked.

I couldn't say yes, because I didn't know if I could, but I couldn't say no, because my father would kill me.

"Follow me," I said, with a twelve-year-old's poise and presence, even as I looked furtively for my mother. She was at the cash register, her glasses on, pressing buttons and moving her lips. She might as well have been behind bars.

We ducked and dodged other customers and made our way to the back of the first floor. We passed the Ship'n Shore blouses; the knit, elastic-waist slacks; the poly-tricot nighties; the brushed flannel pajamas; the acrylic, vinyl-palm gloves; the Poll Parrot and Hush Puppies shoes; the pierced and pierced-look earrings. I could hear my father's voice rise above the crowd. He spent his days waiting for his nights: his book of numbers. To pass the time, he yelled at the help and crooned to the customers.

"Yolanda, I'm a fonda' you," he sang to a customer, as she waited her turn at the cash register. "Eugenie, give me a penny and I'll give you a dollar bill." To my father, lyrics were kindred spirits to numbers. They had to fit and have the right number of syllables. "Daisy, Shmaisy, give me your answer do. I'm half crazy, give me eight, twenty-two."

"That Mr. Schmurr got a perpetual song in his blessed heart," Verna said as we made our way through the umbrellas and car coats. She told me she needed a new bra for her niece's christening and right away I pictured girls in bridal-like gowns, boys in blue suits, and Verna Pixley in a new, bright-white Playtex.

At every step in that walk to the back of the store, we sank or bumped or floated into other customers' arms or hips or bottoms. This was the three o'clock rush when the rubber workers of U.S. Rubber emptied into Schmurr's. They were line workers, front-line footwear workers who assembled rubber boots and U.S. Keds. They had fifteen minutes to either grab a donut next door at the coffee shop or come to us to buy pastel shells or housecoats or half-aprons. When fifteen minutes was up, a whistle blew that you could hear clear down Rubber Avenue and the workers had to race back to their line. To save time, I thought, they must pee in their pants.

Fifty, sixty, seventy women filled Schmurr's during the three o'clock rush. Men came in too, but not in such masses, not with such panic or dogged purpose. Our Men's department upstairs was smaller and had mostly work pants for rubber workers, painters' pants for painters, pants for the safety pin and lipstick tube workers, pants for the mechanics, the chemists, the bottle makers, the candy makers, and the mayor. The women were the bread and butter of Schmurr's. My father understood that women had abundant and abiding buying potential. They needed to dress as workers and wives; as housekeepers, cooks, and food shoppers; as mothers, gardeners, and car drivers; as party, beach, and churchgoers. They got old and sick and needed to buy things that slipped on easily, that didn't need buttoning. They needed proper dress for luncheons and club meetings. They bought novelty items, things they didn't know they needed: furry slippers and nighties with French travel phrases. They got pregnant. They got fat. And they filled every inch of Schmurr's with noise, heat, and smell. They filled it with their bodies, mostly big, hot bodies, so many bodies my own body felt unnecessary and weightless. In the rubber worker rush on Schmurr's, I became disembodied, which was what I really wished for then.

If I were bodiless, I wouldn't have to take gym. Without a body, I wouldn't have to take off my clothes in the girls' shower.

Just that day, the day Verna Pixley entered our store, I was working on a problem having to do with taking off my clothes in the girls' locker room. Initially, this seemed a mathematical problem that could only have a mathematical solution. To get credit for gym class, we had to take off all our clothes and get in the gang shower. Now, none of us twelve-year-olds wanted to reveal our bodies—either to ourselves or to others. On the other hand, we wanted credit for jumping jacks, half pushups, half sit-ups, running our half-court basketball. So, what to take off; how to take it off; how to be naked without being naked; how to get wet while remaining dry.

Math failed me, so I went on to magic, logic, mechanical engineering. It was really about magic, so I worked the problem magically, picturing myself simultaneously dressed and undressed, dry and wet, and leaving the gang shower wrapped in a big towel and eligible for credit. Now, if I didn't get credit for taking a shower I'd get a failing grade, a sixty-five, and my father, looking at my report card for two short seconds, would see before him the ninety-five, the ninety, the eighty-five, the eighty, and invite that sixty-five to stick in his craw.

What's with the sixty-five? What about gym? he'd say, pointing to the sixty-five with the neat nail of his index finger. *You need to be fit. Fit's important. Fit's the most important thing. Look at my bicep. Look!* It was a big bicep, marbled with veins. It looked like a snow igloo bursting at the seams with a big, extended family inside. He worked at this. There were hand weights and hand grips and arm stretchers in the master bathroom. At parties or casual dinners with friends, he won more arm-wrestling matches and did more one-handed pushups than any other man. He'd get redder in the face, moan louder, push more. He had the biggest veins and biggest biceps and I had to be naked in the girls' shower to win his approval.

What's your excuse? he would say, his now-relaxed arm pointing again at the sixty-five. There was no excuse and the only way to survive in the world was to have no body. It all came down to having an invisible body, denying the body, or trying to just walk away from the body, leaving the shell behind and taking the head with you.

But for now, tunneling through the crowd with Verna Pixley, I needed my body and it was there for me, even though it felt slight and light as air. The girls—Lena, Theresa, Esther, Martha, Rita—each with different customers, looked at me with badly restrained smiles. I was a new act for the ongoing show of their lives, which often seemed purposeless and unending. When my segment was over and the rubber worker rush was gone, they'd go back to sizing, sorting, and straightening the same clothes they'd been handling for months. They were heroic by default and necessity.

If by excruciating boredom they didn't fold a sleeve under a sweater or left uncorrected a size 16 mixed in with the 18s, my father could sniff it out like a Bullmastiff and come out of his cubicle with his snout in a state of agitated expectation. He'd approach the sweater bin, stiffen his body, lower his chin, and bark, *What pain in the ass isn't doing her job?*

Finally, at the far corner of the first floor, Verna and I reached a cramped section close to the back exit. The size of a 1950s closet, it was not big enough to qualify as a department unto itself. Among ourselves, we called the section simply, *Bras*. On wooden shelves painted a deep aqua—the same paint we used on our aqua-colored ranch house—the bra boxes were stacked in uneven rows. They looked like books in the library. On the bra boxes I saw a mass of numbers and letters, a kind of Dewey decimal system I hadn't yet learned. There were also pictures of women in bras from which I could determine the style—whether the straps had lace, for example, or whether there was a floral design on the cups. But the picture couldn't tell me if the bra had a light liner or big pads or what-the-hell-size this huge Verna Pixley would wear. What the pictures—white women with pointed nipples and neat pageboys—told me was this: you couldn't opt out of breasts. You couldn't get a written excuse; you couldn't be out that day.

"Playtex Cross Your Heart is nice," I said, mimicking my mother. "It lifts and separates." She looked at me like I was nuts.

"Lifts and separates," I said again, holding my hands out like a book, then raising them up and out. It was a gesture Moses might have made to part the Red Sea. I had no idea what I was saying. Lift and separate sounded like something a bulldozer did to shale and rock.

"Oh yeah!" she said, suddenly, startling me. "I saw that commercial on TV. Playtex lifts and separates. That's right. Right. Good."

She was with me and I was with myself until I asked again, "What size?"

"Size big-as-you-got."

"Sorry, but I need a number," I said. "We need to get it right because bras are not returnable. That's a state law, not Schmurr's." I felt I was a spiritual medium and my dead grandfather, the screw and retail magnate, was speaking through me.

I looked up at some big numbers I saw on the bra boxes. "Forty-two, forty-four?"

"Lordy," she said. "It been so long. Can you read the tag on the bra I'm wearin'?"

And before I had the chance to scream, she had her shirt up in the back of the store as though the words "private parts" meant nothing to her.

Well, I would have needed a map to find that tag, the expanse of bra was so big and the terrain so diverse. On her back were both raised and recessed spots, dots and scars. And the bra itself was in places bumpy or smooth, threadbare or thick, heavy or light, white or beige according to various stretch, pull, or tension points. I found where the straining hook eyes came together but I had no room and not enough strength to flip the material over to find the tag.

"I can't find it," I said.

To which she replied, "I'll just take off the whole thing then." I must have had the look of a lean, nervous sprinter waiting for the gun to go off because she said to me, "Look, baby, I need this bra. Your daddy says in his jingle, tell us what you need and we get it for ya. I got less than five minutes. If I'm late, they kill me."

We were both living with death threats—she from her supervisor, me from my father if I failed to make, or tried to make, this sale. "Go in the dressing room," I said quietly, "and take off your bra."

I looked high up on the shelf and saw forty-twos, forty-fours, but then there were the cup sizes, the Cs, the Ds, the CCCs, or the DDDs, the wired and not wired, the laced and plain, the cotton straps or stretch straps, the black or white. I was going for a forty-four DD when she called out from the dressing room. "Little Girl! I found the tag but it's so old I can't read it. Maybe forty-four! Quick. Just get me forty somethin'."

I pulled a forty-six DDD from the shelf and ran to the dressing room.

There in the tiny closet of a room, I nearly drowned. For Verna stood before me naked from the waist up, with breasts as big and obscene as anything I could ever have imagined. The full-length mirror made me see four breasts, and for a moment the four nipples, like four wide puckery mouths, sucked all the oxygen out of the room, and it seemed I was breathless and floating. "See about this," I said, almost throwing the bra box at her while trying to run out, but she said to me, "Girlie girl, I'm afraid I be too sweaty to try these on. You got some paper towel, sweet pea? Or just a rag?"

Then and there I must have made a decision, a heartfelt promise to heaven that for a "girlie girl" or "sweet pea" I would do anything for her. My father gave me names like *pisspot*, *whiner*, names of horses that would never win the Kentucky Derby.

But Verna's names for me were loving, tender. She didn't even know me and she was probably going to be docked money for returning late to her line. I ran for rags. What I found was a new roll of toilet paper in the utility closet and some baby powder. I grabbed them both and ran back. I unwrapped, unrolled, sprinkled, mopped, and felt like a true professional in the field.

"That's good, honey doll," she said to me, as I was balling up paper, rubbing her down. "That's good, sweet plum. Nice, baby, nice, nice." She pointed her index finger down her back. "Below the shoulder blade, lemon drop. That's good." Her tone worried me a little, but I was so in love with the promise of other fruit she had yet to call me that I just went on with my rubbing and mopping. "How'd you learn to be such a good helper?" she asked me.

"My mother's teaching me but . . ." I knew I should just shut up and make a sale, but I wanted to tell her. Even though she was half naked, I edged slightly closer to her face and looked into her ear as I spoke. "I think I'm bad at bras," I said.

Her whole body seemed to tighten. She crossed her legs at the ankles and bent way over, her breasts approaching the floor way before the rest of her came close. "You're not bad at nothin', sweetheart. Only don't make me laugh. I'll pee in my pants."

"Don't do that," I said. "We'll have to get you underwear, too, and I don't understand underwear, either."

"Don't understand underwear?" Still bent over, she put one hand on her stomach and the other hand straight out, as though she was trying to stop traffic. "Don't make me laugh!" But she laughed. She couldn't help herself. And she peed. "Wait 'til you have your babies," she said to me. "You start leaking now and then."

Leaking. No one told me about leaking.

"I got 4 minutes," Verna said.

She had started trying on the bras, now that I had prepped her, and I went to look for "dry panties," as they say in lingerie. Luckily, I ran into my mother, who was trying to make some order in the back-snap dresses.

"Ma!" I yelled. "I got some lady trying on a bra! Forty-six DDD."

"You poor thing," she said.

"And she needs underwear, too! I haven't learned the underwear!"

"I'll get it. I'll get extra big—triple X—and meet you back there."

Verna almost had the bra on, but needed me to hook it. As the two hook-eyes came together, she said, "Yes, Yes, baby. Good! Good!"

I felt I'd come in first, whatever it was I had entered. Then there was a knock on the dressing-room door. "Who is it?" I asked, resenting the intrusion with my customer.

"Just me," said my mother. She opened the dressing room door and I saw a hand enter, a disembodied hand from which was dangling industrial-size panties. I grabbed them, gave them to Verna. "Meet me at the cash register," I told her.

I was sorry to leave her. I would have helped her put on her blue sweat-soaked jersey and her black stretchy pants. I think she was sorry to see me leave, too. "Yes, darlin'," she said.

I walked down the front aisle to the cash register carrying her old bra, the new bra box, and the price tag from her new pair of panties. My mother saw me and cheered.

"Atta way, babe." The girls—Lena, Theresa, Esther, Martha, Rita— stood behind the counter, their bodies like packages they had wrapped in their own arms. I felt I was approaching a receiving line of New York aunts. Their faces, happy now as they saw me, were ready to snap into boredom at a moment's notice. The old bra hung from my hand like cascading babies' breath. My face was flushed. Verna was behind me now, calling, "Where's my baby girl? Where's that girl child?"

"Her name's *Ellen,*" my mother called out from behind the cash register.

Beside her, my father was crooning, "Somewhere, over the rain hats," to a small white woman as he rang up her triangular plastic babushka. As I walked down the aisle he saw me, witnessed my victory, felt the spirited air around him, and interrupted his song to belt out an insult so everyone could hear. "That's my pain in the ass."

I was twelve, but at that moment I was pushed further out, over my head. And while I didn't ask for retail, I knew, for better and for worse, it was beginning to happen to me. My father knew it, my mother knew it, and Stuart, having just now finished practice in the fall dusk, likely knew it, too. Retail was the woman I'd soon become.

Miss McCook

THE DAY I MOVED, my father was indignant. In his coat and hat, scarf and gloves, he paced the new, bare rooms. He raised and lowered shades, ran water, gripped the knobs on doors and pulled. Then he walked out.

I found him, his eyes shut, sitting in the Lincoln. I knocked on the window by the driver's seat but he didn't answer. I knocked hard, my hand in a fist, my fingertips pressed in my palm. He didn't look up so I got in on the passenger side. His eyes were still shut, the heat was on high. On the tape deck, Leontyne Price screamed an aria from *Aida*. I shouted above her. "Dad!"

He lowered the music and opened his eyes. "The kitchen smells like cat piss, the bathroom smells like cat piss, and what if there's a fire?"

"I'll run. I can run fast."

"She'll run. Flames everywhere and she'll run."

"There's a fire escape outside the bedroom window."

"The fire escape looks good for nothing. Good for cat piss."

Like the princess who slept on forty beds and felt the buried pea, my father could sleep on forty beds and smell the buried pea. And smell the cat beneath the pea. He smelled cats whenever I left home—in my tents at camp, my rooms at college. Don't listen to him, my mother always said. When has he ever smelled a cat? He grew up with dogs. Right, he'd say, agreeing with her so he could catch her off guard. And then I married your mother.

I was leaving home again. I'd come home in May, after graduating from college. We all knew it was a temporary stay; in December I would start my first job, move to my first apartment. For six months my mother went through boxes: Can you use slotted spoons? Grapefruit spoons? Ellen? Are you sleeping? For six months I lay in bed but I wasn't sleeping. I was practicing the cannonball dive. I hugged my thighs to my chest, I pressed my head to my knees, I held my breath. My bed was the bluff, the floor was the sea.

My mother lifted my covers to show me her spoons and I inspected them by bringing them inside, running my thumbs along the metal. Thank you, I said, my voice blocked by tops of boxes popping. Do you think you'll fondue? Ellen? Squeeze an orange? Never mind that, my father said. She needs wrenches and nails. And is this place safe, I want to know. Hello? Ebullient El? You have good locks on this apartment? The door secure?

"Yes."

"Don't say yes unless you're sure."

"I'm sure."

"Wise guys are sure. Smart guys are cautious. Hello? Eloquent El? You cautious?"

Under the covers, I felt the spoons. They were warm as my skin. Warm as my knees touching my chin.

"Hello?" My mother knocked on the windshield. "The movers are ready. What should I tell them?"

I turned to my father. It was his answer she was waiting for. He lowered the heat, raised the music. She knocked on the windshield again. "Irv? Irv?"

He left the car and walked down the street. His open coat flew out like a flag.

"They're impatient," she called out. "What should I tell them?"

He hugged the coat to his chest. "Tell the bastards to be careful."

I was a fifth-grade teacher, the successor to Mrs. McCook, who in December took a maternity leave. The children missed McCook. Instead of watching my slides on Frederic Remington and the North American Indian, they made cards and gifts for McCook's new baby. They called me Miss McCook.

It wasn't easy stepping into her shoes. I didn't like the reading or math texts she used. I didn't like the mirror she hung on the wall (it lured children out of their seats, enticed them to stare, to pull their hair and lips, kiss themselves, kiss the glass). I couldn't understand her seating plan. She seemed to have ordered children by sexual maturity. Girls were arranged by descending breast size: big breasts were in the back, emerging breasts in the middle, flat breasts closest to me in the front. The girls in the back were altogether big for their age, tall as well as full, and they sat too close to the small timid boys who McCook, inexplicably, also placed in the back. The biggest boys with the biggest mouths sat front-row center—perhaps a ploy of McCook's to keep them from shouting. They shouted nonetheless and their voices, so close to me, assaulted my ears. "McCook!" they screamed. "How you grow so short?"

"It's Schmurr, Miss Schmurr."

"Shirt!" they screamed. "How you kiss your man? You stand on the roof? On the clouds? You hang from the sky?"

If a big, tall girl liked a small, timid boy, she'd slap his cheek, touch his mouth, move up close and murmur, "ugly face, ugly face." If a loudmouthed boy liked a flat-breasted girl he'd grab her arm and pin it to her back, all the while hunching over her, pressing in.

"McCook! I'm going to save my money and take you to dinner!"

"Miss Schmurr. And be smart. Buy a book with your money."

"Buy a book! Rather buy me a ham! Or some fuzzy fun!"

"Fuzzy fun!" screamed a big girl in the back row. "What lady want your dollar bill?"

"Buy a smoked ham," I said. "Or a dictionary. Buy a dictionary."

"Shirt, what you give me if I buy a dictionary?"

"Yah, Shirt. What you give me if I do all my work?"

Behind McCook's desk I stared at them. I wanted to give them what they'd lost. They were not much older than ten. They had their whole lives to lose it again.

I couldn't smell cats in my kitchen. But I didn't know how a cat smelled. I grew up with dogs. To be safe, I flooded the floor with ammonia. "Tell me what you smell," I said to my neighbor Glen.

"Ammonia."

He had a nose in the real world. And a foot in the door, my kitchen door, where he stood and watched me work. I mopped and sponged. I wrung rags. I used brushes, steel wool, razor blades.

Glen lived across the hall and his proximity to me gave him special rights: to get familiar fast, to stand like a rack in my doorway. I didn't like being watched. His shoulders were too attentive. They leaned forward to follow me, rocked when I stopped to rest. I didn't rest often.

"Where do you get your energy?" he asked, watching me work a stain.

"When you doing *my* floor?" he asked, rolling the sleeves of his green flannel shirt.

"You're making me feel guilty," he said, his shoulders set in shame.

So go home, I wanted to say. But couldn't. Instead I tried pretending he wasn't there. I wasn't successful. His large figure flashed on the wet kitchen floor and everywhere I looked I saw green.

. . .

The man didn't come through the door. He came up the fire escape and through the bedroom window. At 6 a.m., awakened by the winter air, I strained to understand: an open window, a sneaker, a fragment of leg; an open window, a sneaker, the leg growing longer. This wasn't a still life I could study: a pear, a lemon, an egg. It was a moving sneaker and a moving leg. A window wide open. I sat up and wrapped myself in sheets. "Bastard!" I screamed. "Bastard! Bastard, Bastard!" My screams were gunfire. They got him in the leg, in the heart. They got him where it hurt. And he fled.

"I never saw his face," I said to the officer. He leaned against my bedroom wall and filled out a form.

"I didn't see his age, race, height." The cop lit a cigarette, took a drag, held his breath.

"He wore a high, white sneaker." He rubbed his back against my wall and left a smear of blue.

"His leg was smallish." His hips were thick with holster and gun.

"I screamed, he left." He exhaled his smoke in the edge of my robe.

I made up contact rules: "There shall be no grabbing, hitting, punching, kissing during math, spelling, or science. When I take aside a reading group neither—you hear that—neither . . ."

"I hear—beaver, beaver!"

"Neither the people in the group nor the people at their desks may touch the leg of another."

The rules made them edgy. Like tiny Talmudic scholars they wiggled and rocked in their seats. They ate fire balls by the bushel. They screamed even louder than usual.

"Got you last night!"

"You did not get me!"

"Got your sister in the Bank Street alley!"

"You did not get my sister!"

"Got your mother! Got her on your front porch steps!"

"You did not get my mother! Her boyfriend got her!"

"I got her, too!"

"You got shit, Shamont!"

I wouldn't sleep. Instead of closing my eyes I kept watch over my window. I sat propped up on pillows, my night light on. Beneath my bed were arms—a can of mace, a wrench, a planter hook with a jagged claw. I considered who he might be. Maybe Mark, my boyfriend in college. Maybe he drove cross-country just to climb my fire escape, catch me in my sleep. He had a motive; he always said I didn't love him. He lived with his parents who were always around. And peculiar. His mother left pots of uncovered stew on the stove which the cats sniffed and pawed. The stew collected dust by day and by night became dinner. The whole family—even the father—watched *Star Trek* while they ate, and the house hadn't been cleaned in years. We made love in the basement, on a rollaway covered with hair. Upstairs I could hear his parents talking. If the pitch of their voices rose, I froze and could only go so far. "Relax," he'd say. "They're probably doing the same thing." "Right," I'd say. "Now I can relax." My back itched. I saw webs on the wall.

"McCook! You going to have a baby like Miss McCook?"

"Who am I?"

"Something like Shirt?"

I held my hand under my chin. "Notice, if you will, my likeness to myself."

"Miss McCan! Miss BigCan!"

"Miss Schmurr. Say it. Miss Schmurr."

"Miss Shirt!"

"Again."

"Miss Shirt! Say it! Again! Miss Shirt! Say it! Again!"

They chanted, profaned, chanted, profaned, and shortly thereafter forgot my name.

. . .

He was just some man, loose-limbed, nimble-jointed, just a little desperate and out of his mind and looking for sex. He was ready to give himself—to anyone, anything, it didn't matter. He was ready to fall in love. He fell in love with my fire escape and began climbing.

Bastard be nimble / Bastard be quick / Bastard climbs my fire escape / And so too climbs his wick.

And so too climbs his sneaker.

And on whose foot will the sneaker fit? A joiner? A doer? A banker? A sailor? A cowboy? A ploughboy? A lover? A son?

If I dozed for a while then woke, my room seemed strange. I couldn't name things. My parents' old bureau was a mound of brown, a square blot. My lamp and chair were lines and squares, foreign bodies. Through my open closet door, I saw slacks and skirts and knew they were clothes, but they didn't seem to belong to me. I didn't seem to belong to me. I couldn't name myself.

I couldn't tell my parents about the break-in; they'd insist I move home. Insist all you want, I'd say as I packed.

At home I would sleep. But it wouldn't be restful. Like an agitated professor, my father would walk circles around my bed.

I knew the place was a come-on, a crime trap. But does anyone listen to her father? Does anyone say, Dad, you're a learned man, I want to cash in on your wisdom. I knew it was just a matter of time before something happened. You're an eligible young victim, El. And the world, let me stress, is full of opportunists. There are men of vision, if you will, who can look through a wool coat, a wool sweater, a set of thermal underwear and still see weakness. You have to be on your guard. Ellen? Are you listening? Wake up. Learn to protect yourself. Learn to be a wolf.

Don't listen to him, my mother would say. Be yourself.

Be a wolf in sheep's clothing, if you want.

Be who you are.

She's a sleeping paschal lamb, about to get lanced.

· · ·

I told Glen about the break-in. I told him that I couldn't sleep. One night he came over with a power drill. We stood side by side in my bedroom. "You need to secure your window," he said. I watched his reflection as he guided the drill into the frame.

"I didn't ask for this break-in," I told his reflection.

"You think I think you did?"

"Talk slowly. I'm tired. Things don't make sense."

"You think. I think. You did?"

I still didn't follow but said no and hoped it was the right answer.

We were both wearing flannel, the material of friendly neighbors. In the window, his shoulders looked like wings. The drill, tiny in his hands, was an egg. I was a baby finch in flannel. He put penny nails into the holes he drilled. "The window is secure now, see?" He tried to lift it, he pulled on it hard, but it stayed in place. "No one'll come in."

"What?"

"No one. Will come. In."

"Oh. No one will come in."

"Miss Echo."

"Miss Schmurr."

That night, the window nailed tight, I sat guard until the sun rose. I added a rolling pin to the collection under my bed. I was stockpiling arms to ensure my peace.

Sleep was all we talked about.

"If you can't sleep alone," he said, "stay with me."

"I don't want to sleep."

"Everybody wants to sleep. Sleep is necessary."

I needed rest, I told him, not necessarily sleep. My mother used to tell me to rest if I couldn't sleep. As long as you lie still, she said, the body can repair itself. This made me think I was undetectably marred and gouged and I lay perfectly still hoping to be healed.

· · ·

He was a scared cat, a cocky hare, a ne'er-do-well snail always getting short shrift. He was a wounded wolf with a burr in his paw. His hurt was so great, his haunches collapsed and he crawled down the street on his belly. He crawled down the boulevard, passed Phil's Deli. He was looking for some lamb to remove the burr. That's all. He hadn't expected to feel turned on. But the rubbing of his belly against the ground got the best of him. It got him so bad his eyesight failed and when in the distance he saw a fire escape it looked like an outstretched, helping hand. He crawled to the hand and began climbing.

I marked off sleepless nights as if charting my cycle. I was McCook counting the days of her missed period. I counted seven, fourteen, twenty-one. I was one month sleepless. One month crazy. At school, I felt disembodied. There was the me who taught and the me who dangled from the ceiling watching me teach. I watched as I taught the children to make animals out of colored paper. We folded and folded until we had the likeness of wild game. I listened to myself give instructions: "We are in the jungle. The hunters are after our animals. Let's help them escape. Write messages on them and fly them out the window. Set free the rabbits and quail. Set free the fishes and buffalo. Say good-bye to them."

"Bye Dirty Bird!"

"Bye Dirty Dog!"

Bye McCook, McWick, McWolf.

I watched as I allowed children to go to the lavatory, not one at a time but in twos and fours, in mixed company. I watched as they returned twenty, thirty minutes later, returning in twos and twos. In mixed company. I stared with interest as I walked to the door to greet the principal. He held in one hand a paper hen.

"Miss Schmurr. Why are your children throwing things out the window?"

"We're celebrating the coming of spring," I lied.

"It's January."

"Right."

"Are you aware that the writings on these things are obscene?"

"No, sir." His thumb was covering the writing on the hen but I knew what it said. "Suck Cock." I wrote that message myself.

"And a more serious offense—why were a boy and a girl from your class allowed to enter a utility closet?"

"They weren't in the lav?"

"They weren't in the lav, they didn't have passes, it took the hall monitor fifteen minutes to get the door opened. I punished the children but we have to—Miss Schmurr? Are you listening? You look like you're not listening."

I met with him after school and told him I was tired and not myself. We've already lost one teacher in the class, he told me. We don't want to lose another. He told me to take a week's leave and get some sleep.

I stood outside Glen's apartment wrapped in a wool blanket. One side of it slipped off my shoulder when I knocked on the door.

"I have blankets," he said, as I walked into his living room. He stood at the stove in the half kitchen. I saw him through the large cut-out square which separated one room from the other. He was stirring a spoon in a saucepan. "I'm making you strong warm milk. It'll make you so sleepy you won't know what hit you."

"What what?"

"What hit you."

I kept the blanket around me and sat on the couch.

"See how bumpy it is? You take the bed."

"You take the bed."

He poured the milk in a mug that said *Glen*. "You can have the Glen mug."

"What will you use?"

"I have two Glen mugs." He poured himself a mug of cognac, poured cognac into my milk, and joined me on the couch. "What's the longest you ever slept?" he asked me.

"I don't know. A few months? I sleep to avoid things. What about you?"

"Eighteen hours. I didn't really sleep all that time but I stayed in bed. It was this time I was fucking this woman who was married. And she had to stop seeing me. And I didn't want to stop seeing her. So I got into bed one day and just started thinking about her. I went to bed at three in the afternoon and didn't get up until nine the next morning. I slept, dreamt about her, thought about her, slept."

"Did it help you get over her?"

"No, it helped me hold onto her."

"Fucking. I don't like that word."

"I loved her. But I knew it was wrong. So, I call it fucking."

"Some things are wrong," I said, trying to sound wise.

"Some things aren't," he said. He poured more cognac into our mugs and we drank until my neck felt weightless, until I was sure my body, even on the jungle terrain of the couch, could float.

"I think I can sleep now," I said.

"Good." He brought me another blanket and pulled a space heater in front of the couch. "In case you get cold," he said, and kissed the top of my head. He went into his bedroom and I heard him opening drawers, moving a chair. I heard water running. I turned on the space heater.

"You okay?" he called out.

"Yes."

The heater hummed and warmed me. I dozed, dreamt I was dozing, dreamt I opened my eyes. I opened my eyes. Glen's couch was not just bumpy; it had its own arsenal. Beneath the cushions, I felt an egg beater, a wire whisk, a serving spoon. I lay in a curl on my side, I practiced the tuck of the cannonball dive, I tried to doze. But couldn't. I felt hot from the heat of the heater, I turned the heater off. Without the hum the room seemed darker. I turned on the light.

"Ellen? What's going on?"

"Nothing. I'm not sleeping."

He came into the living room, walked to the couch, sat in the space of my curl. "You've given *me* insomnia." His wrap-around robe was a doe-colored beige. I watched as I pinched the terry cloth cord and pulled.

"What are you trying?" he asked, running a finger down my cheek. "What are you saying?" he asked, prying the blanket away from my fist. "Hmmm? Tell me."

"I only want some sleep."

We slept for three consecutive days. By the fourth I thought maybe I was in love. By the fifth I was looking for an apartment on a safer side of town.

Glen suggested I move in with him, then noticed the look on my face. "Right," he said.

My father suggested I was crazy. "What are you? Crazy? You just moved." The static on the phone had the sound of the sea.

"The place is a fire trap," I told him.

"Now you're talking," he said. I imagined I had a conch shell pressed to my ear. "And that fire escape looks good for nothing." His voice was the voice of a father, whispering above the waves.

I returned to school on dress-up day. Wearing their best, the children kept a clean, wide distance from each other. Their good clothes quieted them and they screamed softer than usual. They screamed at me, their teacher, who returned to school in a secondhand dress and a stole of fake fur.

"Shirt! Who you supposed to be?"

"Miss Schmurr."

"Shirt don't dress like that!"

"No? How does she dress?"

"She wear big, long skirts!"

"Good. What else?"

"She be wearing flat, black shoes!"

"Good. What else?" Hands were waving.

"She got this big bangle bracelet she sometime wear!"
"She wear white blouses!"
"And gold dot earrings!"
"And she never wear makeup!"
"Not even blush!"
And there I was.

Harvester

IN THOSE SIX years following college, I had just one employer—New York University. And for three of those years, I had just one boy-friend—Ted. He was a cameraman, always in and out of work. During one hiatus, he hurt his back playing racquetball, and gradually—so gradual I didn't see it coming—he fell in love with his back pain.

At the end of the day, I'd come home to our studio and he'd be in bed lying on his hydrocollator—a gray pad he endlessly boiled in our spaghetti pot. He'd use a big pair of wooden tongs to remove the pad; then he'd lie on it until it got cold. After a while, he'd cook it up again. Our studio was always filled with steam.

Back then I was a research assistant to Professor Waxman, who was studying ways to desensitize people to night fears. For each subject, I had to play a relaxation tape, then show a film that got progressively darker. On day one, you saw a bed and a bureau in bright light, and by day five you could barely see anything at all, except the illuminated red hands of an alarm clock. I had to conduct interviews in which I asked subjects to describe their worst fears. It was amazing what people were afraid of. It was unsettling how descriptive they could be.

Ted didn't want to hear about it. And he could only talk about whether he felt tighter or looser; employable, unemployable; more bummed, less bummed. The hydrocollator took up more and more room in our bed; the bed took up most of the space in our studio; our spaghetti pot was never used for a meal.

Finally, he smoked me out. Which was okay. I had friends. I had my job. Only now I was afraid of the dark.

"New shirt?" Professor Franzi asked. I was in my sixth year as a research assistant at NYU and was considering a move. Maybe the NYU financial aid office or NYU fundraising or recruiting. "New scarf?" Professor Franzi asked. He didn't know new from old. He had just been appointed in the political science department, and I'd just started working for him. I told him things about NYU. I explained the benefits to him—the sick and vacation days, the health plan, the pension and flexible spending program. I showed him how the coffee maker worked. He learned fast, and he noticed things. He noticed when I trimmed my hair, had fresh paper in my notebook. He smiled when I walked in his office, smiled when I left. He took off his glasses when we spoke. He took off his glasses when he fired me.

"He laid me off," I said to Todd, my boyfriend of seven months. "I can't believe it." Todd lived in Connecticut and when I spoke to him by phone I always felt I was communicating with the real world. Not a cameraman or a professor. Just a guy—a blond prince of the normal people. "I can't believe it," I said. "People have always liked my work. I've always been considered an asset, a good worker."

"You are an asset," Todd said. "But you have to remember something. Franzi is a fuck-up. Forget about him. Come live with me."

My job had been to read newspaper stories during Lyndon John-son's presidential campaign and put the content into a numerical code. Specifically, I had to read and analyze every story that had to do with the Cold War. "Goldwater Uses Red Issue," for example, might be 5-5-2-1.

I scrolled my way through miles of microfiche. I squeezed a million numbers onto computer sheets. I ate scores of Jujubes to stay awake. After I coded a batch of stories, Professor Franzi would take my num-bers and feed them into his computer.

He seemed to like my work at first. He certainly seemed to like talking to me. He liked Czech food, he said. Hearty pheasant. Black bean soup. He wore sweaters with horizontal stripes to make his shoul-ders looked broader. Did I like Czech food, he wanted to know? The rugged breads? Yes, I said. I did.

Three weeks later, he called me into his office. He hadn't liked the numbers he was seeing and wanted to know if I was "on track." His smile started to droop. "How would you code this *Times* story about Humphrey's campaign speech in Detroit?" He had in front of him a copy of the story. "This is the one where Humphrey blasts Barry Gold-water for saying Johnson was soft on communism."

"6-0-0-5," I said.

We were sitting side by side in office chairs and he leaned closer to me, pointing to a paragraph at the top of the page. "The one," he said, "where Humphrey says, *If Goldwater has to dig up that old smelly argument...?*"

"Right," I said. "6-0-0-5."

Franzi moved away from me and pointed farther down. "The one where Humphrey says, *Barry Goldwater will die in the stench of his own political argument?*"

"Yes," I said with conviction. "6-0-0-5."

"5? I would have said, 6-0-0-3."

"3? I wouldn't have said 3. If anything, 4-0-0-5."

"4? 4?"

So we had major philosophical differences, the upshot being he couldn't work with me.

"You couldn't work with *him*," Todd said. His shoulders looked broad no matter what he wore.

"You have to think of skills you can transfer to another job," Todd said over the phone. "Preferably in Connecticut. Preferably starting out each morning from my house."

I looked around where I was, my tiny, post-Ted apartment on 44th Street. The couch folded out into a single bed. A bureau next to the stove was stuffed with silverware and winter sweaters. The night stand next to the couch had canned goods in the bottom drawer.

"6-0-0-5, Todd," I said. "It's not really a traveling show."

"Look for what that job has in common with other jobs. Jobs outside academia. Claims investigator. Fact checker."

"A spy."

"Okay, maybe intelligence work, investigative work."

"A spy whose boss betrays her," I said.

"Ruth, you had one bad experience. Not a lifetime of them."

"You haven't known me for my lifetime."

I stared at an oriental screen which had become my pushpin bulletin board. On a backdrop of robed women holding bonsai branches, I had pinned posters of NYU foreign films, NYU exhibits, NYU concerts and lecture series. "Franzi cut me off, Todd."

"You'll grow back stronger."

"He put me on a lily pad. Then severed the stem."

"You overexaggerate."

"I'm floating away."

"Float over to my house."

"I'm melting."

"Melt outside my door."

"Have some coffee ready. And maybe a little Danish."

"Deal," he said.

. . .

I moved in with Todd. He had a house, a yard, a job, a dog, a car. I could live with that. He liked to brush my hair, as though putting in place what he understood me to be. I'm not sure what that was, what he saw, but he seemed to like it. He kissed it a lot.

Soon after I moved in, I woke one morning to find Todd in the kitchen drawing an outline of his dog, Rose. Rose was curled up on a piece of white cardboard and Todd was circling her with a carpenter pencil.

"This is different," I said. "We used to trace our hands."

"I'm taking her measurements," he said. "So I can build a doghouse." Todd drew her sitting up and lying down. From her reclining position, Rose stared at him languidly and licked her chops. To her this was not construction, but massage—in the same family as a belly rub. "I don't want her underfoot when you're doing your job hunt."

Todd had bought me all kinds of books and skill inventories for my job conversion. He pampered me with legal pads, showered me with self-help questionnaires.

He finished his sketches and took out a yardstick to measure the lines. It was July and hot in the kitchen, but he still wore long, white carpenter pants and a thick, leather holster studded with Powerman tools. Rose came over to me and licked my bare feet. My feet seemed to have some element that kept her electrolytes in balance. "Tell her no," Todd said. But at that moment I didn't care what Rose did. I was touched. No one had ever built me a doghouse before.

Todd stayed crouched down, making notations inside the sketches, writing notes along the edges of the cardboard. He erased, looked up, wiped his brow, looked to one side, wrote some more. A decent man, a for-once downright decent man was building me a doghouse. The thought flew around me for a few heady moments, throwing off light, blinking, twinkling. Then it smashed into a windshield.

The gesture just seemed too large, too suspect, too unconditional in its love. Not that I felt altogether unworthy. I just felt Donna.

I felt the doghouse was meant for Donna, that he had made a mistake with her and was trying to fix it with me. I felt Donna and I saw Donna—in the afghan on Todd's bed, in the spider plant in the bathroom still shooting out those unrelenting babies. They themselves had no children, just a three-year marriage. He told me he had loved her. He said that, in all honesty, he still loved her.

"So why did you break up?" It had taken me ages to ask the question. Instead I waited for him to tell me and when that didn't come I nosed around the house while he was at the hardware store or doing farm chores for his father. I did a fair amount of marginal poking in his bureau and the string drawer in the kitchen. When that proved fruitless I tried listening, but Todd wasn't a big talker. He looked like a talker; he looked like a slightly weary, sardonic, 100 percent cotton intellectual who could talk well and wear a pair of shorts—a cross between John Lennon and Tab Hunter. But he wasn't a talker. He talked a little about Donna but he'd talk from the outside in, rather than the other way around. He'd talk about the sofa he had with her, with the sumptuous heaps of needlepoint pillows, or the pine coffee table with the recessed knot where she placed chunky candles. Still, I couldn't get him beyond the knot, underneath the pillows. So, finally I had to ask point-blank, "So, why'd you break up?"

"I don't know," he said.

We were in his bed. Wood rosettes were carved on the tip of the headboard and wood leaves cascaded down the sloping sides as if they were falling. It had been his parents' bed. It had been the bed he shared with Donna. "We just stopped talking," he said.

The box fan in his window was set on "high" and I had to raise my voice to a slightly louder and abnormal pitch. "If you loved her, why didn't you just start talking again?"

"I don't know. We were beyond talking and couldn't seem to get back. I don't know. I was going to school getting my master's and I'd stay up late trying to think up a thesis topic. I remember one morning she found me asleep over a blank notebook, with a glass of Yukon Jack next to me. It must have been my third glass. I remember she said, 'Next time spill some whiskey on the page. At least you'll have a stain to start with.'" He laughed.

"I don't get it."

"And she was taking accounting classes and would stay up late putting numbers in columns."

"I don't get it. Was it something like you were going your separate ways, growing apart? Growing up?" He took off his wire rims and set them on the wood night table.

"I don't know, Ruth. I honestly don't know. Why did Franzi fire you? Why do things happen? Maybe it was a little of 6-0-0-5 versus 6-0-0-4. That kind of thing."

"You saw things differently. You were at philosophical odds with each other. You were basically incompatible even though at first there were some real sparks?"

"No."

He rubbed some sweat off the bridge of his nose, where his glasses hit. "It was just something that caught us both off guard, even though it must have been happening a long time."

"It just snuck up on you?" I said too loudly. I noticed with grim interest that the tiny grids of the box fan were filled with dark, hairy mounds of dirt. The dirt bore a great resemblance to the fine, hairy dirt I'd seen in Ted's oscillating fan and to the luxurious head of dirt in Franzi's air-conditioning unit.

"Yes," he said. "That's it." He looked straight ahead at his blank bedroom wall and his face registered a great deal of thought. His head moved slightly, his hand was cupped over his cheek, and he was frowning. "She took off her shirt on our first date."

"God," I said.

"We were alone in the school newspaper office and she just took off her shirt."

"God."

"Who cares. Who cares who did what when. It's over, Ruth. She's remarried. It's over."

"Right," I said. "Right."

He turned off the light, a clamp-on light attached to the carved roses in the headboard. Not always, but often, he'd turn off the light and we'd sigh and I'd feel I was falling back on myself, dizzy in a swoon. But tonight my limbs felt heavy and I couldn't even put my arm around him. I just kept my eyes open in the dark and waited to see where I was.

It was the end of summer and until Todd had to start teaching again he spent his time working on the doghouse. He measured, cut, nailed, and conferred with carpenters. He conferred quite a bit with his father, a farmer, who lived on the other side of town.

When he was finished, he unveiled the house in the back yard. He threw off a huge horse blanket and launched into his tour. He used words like *Plywood*, *A-frame*, *Thermopane*. "You coughed all around the window?" I asked.

"Caulked. I caulked around the window. Do you like the color?" he asked. He had painted the house red—engine red, the color of emergency vehicles, houses burning. Yes, I said. I did.

Todd's back yard was a big square in a small town I never imagined living in. Naugatuck, Connecticut. The home of Naugahyde. The actual site where washable couch covering was manufactured. When I first met Todd, at a party in Fairfield, I thought he was trying to trick me. Naugatuck.

"No," he said. "Honest."

But I didn't trust him until I asked a mutual friend and she gave me the answer with a straight face. "Naugatuck."

Todd grew up there, went to Naugy High. He still went to Naugy High where he taught World Civ. He'd never left Naugatuck except to go to the University of Bridgeport, but he was worldly: You could say to him, *Truk*, *Balaklava*, *Smolensk*, and he'd know, right away, where to point on the globe.

"There's only one flaw in the whole house," Todd said. He stopped the formal tour and sat down. "Rose hates it." He smiled at me but he didn't look happy. He took off his baseball cap—a man's way of saying, "The fun is over."

"How do you know she hates it?" I asked.

"She won't go near it." Standing above him, I could see a ridge in his hair from where the cap had been. I bent over and tried to fluff up the fine and fair strands, tried to bang out the dent with my fingers.

At my feet, Rose played her favorite game: Rip the Rag. She grabbed the rag in her mouth, held it between her paws, and growled, howled, and ripped the thing into a mass of flyaway threads. She was gray, brown, half terrier, half something else. The terrier in her was the hunter: the part that had the instinct to systematically stalk, stand perfectly still, and then annihilate an old rag.

She was annihilating my new orange sneakers, too, incorporating them into her rag game, spitting on them, growling at them. Todd whacked her and she reluctantly opened her mouth and let the rag go. "Sorry, Ruth," he said, as I surveyed the spit on my sneakers.

"It's okay," I said, rubbing the spit around so the tip of my toe was a uniform wet color. "Rose is my top dog."

Todd looked down and snapped some grass from the lawn. "What am I?" he asked.

I sat down next to him and wiped the sweat off my forehead. It was a hot day early in September—one of those days that leave you depressed and perspiring. You think it should be fall. You think you should have a job. You think your mother was right—about everything.

"You're top dog, too," I said to Todd, although frankly I wasn't able to concentrate on him. I was thinking about sitting in the NYU periodical room, a quiet room with long wooden tables and thick walls that separated me not just from the Cold War but from the outright murder and mayhem going on elsewhere in the city. I was thinking about the big cushioned chairs where I read about the Red Scare and wrote small numbers in the tiny squares of computer sheets. I had felt like Thumbelina doing her homework in Judge Hardy's study.

"Am I the toppest dog?" Todd asked. "Enough to marry?"

It was too soon to be asking this of me. There were still-unopened cartons of my stuff in his bedroom closet. I hadn't taken out my address book or the white sneakers I wore to work. I hadn't unpacked books, jewelry, or my better line of casual clothes.

I didn't answer him. Instead, I sat there looking at the doghouse trying to find evidence that he'd told me the truth—that, indeed, he had gone all around the window and caulked.

One night Todd showed me old Super 8 movies—reel to reel. He used one of the bare walls in his bedroom as a screen. Part of his intention was, I think, to show me when he was younger, thinner, had long hair. Guys I knew were always taking out old passports and student IDs to show me their long hair, and I always said the obligatory, "Freaky."

Only this wasn't just about hair. I think—although he wasn't aware of it—he wanted me to see Donna, to see Donna move and speak, to see that somebody with perk and spunk found him desirable enough to marry.

So, in a big well-lit square on his bedroom wall, in a kind of window we were peeking through, I saw Donna move and speak. In the movie, they were camping with friends. First, we saw Todd peeking out of the tent. His hair was long and fine, parted in the middle, a Breck Girl without the sheen. "Freaky," I said. Then we saw his old dog, Grace, also with long hair, sticking her head out of the tent. "What a hippie," I said. Then we saw Donna starting a fire outside the tent and yelling, "Who's got a good match?" She had short hair and a perfect, petite body. Beneath her short jacket, she probably had perky and petite breasts.

There was no way to date her, historically speaking. Her hair could be then or now, her jeans could be then or now, her overbite was timeless. There was nothing outrageous or tie-dyed about her to freeze frame her in the seventies. She was an L.L. Bean Everywoman, constantly current, always camping in Freeport with a red anorak and trail boots. "If I had a good match, a really good match," she said, "we'd be golden." The camera stayed focused on her, the camera probably in love with her.

She was crouched down near the fire, her body folded into a compact package you could fit in your pocket. Carry with you forever.

Todd turned off the projector, turned off the lamp on the headboard, and came into bed with me. Only that night I couldn't make love to him.

"Was it the movie?" he asked, in the dark.

"I think so."

"Sorry. I shouldn't have shown it to you."

"Your hair was so long."

"You didn't like it?"

"Yes, I did. You were cute."

"Was it Donna?"

"Yes."

"Well, maybe it's good that you see her, so you're not imagining her and conjuring up something that's way off the mark."

"Like some ugly, awful person where it's so obvious why you divorced."

"She remarried my best friend."

"Don't tell me any more, ok? I'm better off imagining and conjuring."

We just lay there, not moving or talking, both of us on our backs, until he picked up my hand and kissed it. "So, do I look a lot older?"

"No." My eyes were used to the dark now and I turned and looked at him when I spoke. "Although that hair gets in the way of any real comparison. You look more mature now, and handsome. Seasoned."

"Like a cast iron pan." He beat his chest. "Better with use."

It was quiet in his room, after those whacks to his chest. I could hear his clock making slight ticks, and I began to count them; the number of ticks that were released when I inhaled, exhaled, inhaled. I turned to look at him and his eyes were open, too, as though looking at the ceiling he could see the stars. Could get his bearings.

"Don't forget the *Naugy News*," Todd said, as I sat in the kitchen reading the want ads in the *Waterbury American*. Then he went outside with Rose and threw a ham hock inside the doghouse door.

Yesterday he had thrown a knuckle bone and the day before, a half box of dog biscuits, the name-brand kind. Other days he had tried baked eggplant, pigs in a blanket, Chicken Piperade. But Rose wouldn't go in there for her deep-dish meatloaf with the boiled egg in the middle.

"Sorry, Ruth," he said, when he came inside. He threw the ham hock in the trash. "I tried." I was flattered. No man had ever tried this patiently, this hard, this long.

For a month, until the end of September, I spent a good part of my day in Todd's kitchen, drinking coffee and reading want ads. Administrative assistant, teacher's aide, marketing trainee. Rose licked my toes until I offered her something else. My fingers. My cheek. Reading out loud, I used my most reassuring voice, the voice my mother always used with us kids during thunderstorms—upbeat with an undertone of hysteria. "Junior writer," I said to her. "Development assistant. Assistant to the assistant."

Rose licked my coffee cup clean and never left my side. She came with me as I walked, like a confused interloper, through Todd's living room, bedroom, den. She heard what I had to say, got high from my coffee. And as we paced and drank, as we considered this job, that job, love and marriage, we came upon, if not the answers to our questions, at least a piece of the right track.

My methodology was the time-honored practice of progressive desensitization. My subject was Rose. I figured if I worked with her, if I could gradually get her closer to the doghouse, if I could soften the threat and heighten the pleasure, maybe she'd get down on her belly and crawl in.

On Day One, I tore up an NYU T-shirt and placed it a good fifteen yards from the doghouse. Rose wouldn't look at the house; but she was delighted with the rag. She lit into it, ripping and roaring until sparks flew from her mouth; she salivated until my sneakers darkened and sparkled like quartz.

"How's the job hunting going?" Todd asked.

We were in the living room and I was giving him a scalp massage.

I was swirling my fingers through his hair, as though wiping the glass of a misty windshield. Rose sat by my side, one paw on Todd's belly.

"I'm just getting ideas," I said. "I'm figuring out how to transfer my skills."

"Sounds good," he said. His head was in my lap and I was leaning over him. "Do what you think is best." I wanted to keep talking but I didn't know what to say. I put my hands on either side of his neck, feeling for a pulse, a drum beat, the right key of C. "Just remember me," he said.

Who could forget him? He slept by my side at night. By day, he seemed to blush whenever he said my name. As though the sound of it—*Ruth*—was more biblical than he'd bargained for.

We worked slowly. For one full week we stayed at fifteen yards. We were in no hurry and it was October now, a good time to be outside. Todd's back yard had trees that extended far back to the state road and from the dense brush I could hear vibrant, sometimes rhythmical bug sounds and bird calls. This was a whole new life, this natural world.

One day, unexpectedly, I was overcome by the smell of grass. I was happy to be overcome by grass. Ever since I'd graduated college, in fact for most of my adult life, I hadn't smelled grass, and in a moment of simple, sudden realization, I knew I missed it.

When Rose had ripped her way through two T-shirts, a tank top, and a needlepoint pillow, I cut up my NYU sweatpants, and we moved closer—ten yards away.

"There's always Yale," Todd said, "only forty minutes from here." We were in the kitchen making a dish I'd invented from found objects in the refrigerator. He was wearing an old gray T-shirt, worn so thin that in some places you could see just a few gray threads covering a tiny hole, the kind of shirt he'd wear only around the house. A shirt he'd wear only in front of me.

"Not academia," I said. "I don't want to fall into that old trap again."

"Not all professors are a Franzi, but you know that. Maybe academia is just wrong for you now. Trust your instincts."

This was a new thought for me. Trusting instincts was never something I did, never something I trusted. I always thought instincts were for dogs.

I cut up potatoes, onions, carrots, cabbage. Todd watched white rice boil. Steam from the rice rose up and covered his lenses with a moist smudge. Rose had already eaten leftover shepherd's pie and was asleep under the kitchen table. I had an urge to cover her with a blanket.

"There's always paralegal," I said. I wasn't sure what paralegals did but it sounded like something I could do. Paralegal. Almost legal. A stone's throw from the real thing.

"Or maybe teaching," I said. "Public school teaching." I knew what I was doing here. Donna was a teacher. What I was doing was throwing a Donna bone to see what Todd would do.

"You?" he said.

"Why?"

"Nothing. But you're more scholarly than front line. More substance than glitz."

"I could be both. And I don't have to be glitzy."

"No, I know. You'd be great if you wanted to do it. Do you really want to do it?" He sounded worried.

The kitchen was filled with complex and overwhelming smells, nothing I could put my finger on but something vaguely west of Odessa with traces of Warsaw, Berlin, Vilna. Smells I grew up with. Smells that nourished an ample body that could trample, destroy anything perky and petite.

"Maybe I want to do it. Did Donna like doing it?"

"Very much. But she taught math. All she had to do was wear nice clothes and scrawl all over the board."

I gave him a kiss because this answer satisfied me, because aside from his spoken words I clearly heard the subtext: Donna would be bold and free and young enough to take off her shirt. But I had the bigger, fuller, more potentially abundant breasts.

· · ·

I had books to read: *The Best Jobs for the Eighties. New Living Spaces. Marriage and Intimacy.*

But I didn't read them.

Instead, over the next three weeks, almost into November, Rose and I went from ten yards, to eight, to four. She had shredded my sweatpants, so I made new rags for her out of my NYU sweatshirt with the fleece-lined hood. We were making progress. At three yards, she occasionally looked up and into the doghouse, as though she heard voices coming from inside.

By the time we got to two yards, I was running out of old clothes to tear up, and I felt my time was running out. My instincts, in this case, were right on track.

Todd phoned me from school and asked if I'd meet him for lunch. "I need to get away from here," he said. "All these teachers ever do is smoke and find fault with each other." I put Rose in the car and we met at Burnsie's, a diner on Rubber Avenue. Todd had known Freddie Burns for over twenty years. They were in Cub Scouts together, had gone to Salem School and, of course, Naugy High.

"You brought Rosie?" Todd said. We arrived at the same time and parked around the corner from the diner.

"She loves to get out."

I opened some car windows so she'd have some air, and Todd and I walked to Burnsie's. "Ruth," he started, as soon as we sat down, "I'm not sure about you. Sometimes I think you're happy hanging around the house, figuring out your next step, making meals. But more times than I care to think about, I get the feeling you'll slip out the back door and head for the city."

He stopped for a moment to wave hi to Freddie, who was tending the grill. Then he held up two fingers, a kind of men's code, a secret language that meant either: Give me two of the usual, or my girlfriend has the ears of a burro.

"What did I do?"

I had a nervous, shaky feeling and while I hadn't really expected it,

I thought, right—this makes sense. This is it. This is where he finally hands me my pink slip.

"I have to be assured things are okay with us," he said. "That we're on track. Because if we're not, we should either do something about it now or call it quits. I just can't go through this again."

"I don't want to call it quits." My heart was racing. "Why do you think things aren't okay?"

"Because I don't see any real show of interest or commitment. Are you really looking for a job?"

"I can't figure out my personal and professional life at the same time, Todd. It's too much."

"I don't know, Ruth, I just want you to settle in. If it's okay to ask, what are you doing with your time?"

"Research."

"I need to hear more from you. I need to know you're with me. Otherwise, why should we bother?"

A woman placed in front of us burgers with bacon coming out of the sides like spears. Todd took a few bites, but I couldn't even open my mouth. We sat there ten minutes and didn't say anything. Finally, he stood up, put some money on the table. "It's okay," he said. "We'll talk later."

"How can you teach if you're upset?" I asked. He didn't answer. He just walked out.

What would make someone steal a dog? Anger? Revenge? A case of mistaken identity? Rose certainly wasn't a beauty queen. She had too much gray. The hair around her face was flat and lank. She wasn't a dog for show. She was just our dog. Our Rose.

I called the police. I called the pound. I called Todd's father, who met me at the house. I didn't dare call Todd. He was already angry with me.

"I'm a miserable person," I said to Todd Sr. "A scumball." His father had met me at the house, had asked his wife to stay by the phone at their farm. We were sitting at Todd's childhood desk, a small makeshift square, that he now used as a kitchen table.

"Someone stole your dog," Todd Sr. shouted. "Why does that make you a scumball?"

He took from his jacket an envelope of grocery coupons and set them on the table. He was seventy years old and held onto anything of perceived or questionable value.

"Because I brought her to Burnsie's."

"Did you steal her?"

"No."

"Well, you shouldn't take credit for it then." His voice rose in pitch and, to my ear, anyway, he was hollering. "Do you take credit for every stupid thing someone does?"

I didn't answer, hoping he'd just go on.

"If someone wrongs you, or is a stinkin' liar, do you take credit for it?"

He opened the envelope and started setting his coupons on the small table. "Do you use Camay? Thirty cents. Double coupon, sixty."

I nodded.

"If someone does something low-down and dirty, do you take credit for it?"

"I know I shouldn't," I said.

He shook his head. "There's a lot of nuts in the world. Doesn't mean you have to be one. Do you use nonstick cooking spray? Low-salt gouda? Double coupon, eighty cents."

"Yes," I said.

"You're a smart girl. I know that much. And look here. If you use this coupon and fill out this form, you get a box of Milk-Bones. For nothing. And another thing: no one wants that dog. Believe me."

He was right. Todd's mother called to say Vinnie Marek was at Scheide's Gas Station and saw Rose across the street. He figured she was lost or confused, so he put her in his truck and dropped her off at the farm.

She was in a corner of the kitchen when Todd Sr. and I walked in.

She had just finished another bowl of water and her second scoop of cherry vanilla. She seemed tired, but otherwise okay. She smelled like vanilla when I kissed her.

We all figured the crook must have left her by the side of the road after she snarled and, we hoped, bit him.

Todd's mother was busily going through the freezer, trying to find all the venison scraps she'd been saving for Rose. "Is there anything I can get you, honey?" she asked me. I sat there and thought. I moved a wooden salt shaker back and forth on the kitchen table. "Yes," I said, pushing Rose out of the way as I stood up. "A few scoops of hay." Todd Sr. didn't ask me why; he just seemed flattered I wanted something he had to give. He and Rose and I got in the car and drove to the barn. I backed the car up to a big double door and he loaded half a bale into the hatchback. Rose sniffed the hay, then kept her distance. On the ride back to the farmhouse, she tried to maneuver her entire squat body onto my lap, and I had to push her away so I could drive.

"Do you think hay would make a nice bed in a doghouse?" I asked Todd's father.

"Where'd you hear that?" he said.

"I just thought it up."

"Well, you're right." It was cold in the car—Todd's old car, his old Chevette. Todd Sr. played with some knobs on the dash until he got some heat. "Maybe you'd like farming. Todd never did, really." He shrugged. "Maps, foreign places. That's what he's always liked." He looked out the window and had that look on his face, like Todd, as though he could almost make out the mountains of Luzern, the huts of Truk.

I dropped him off at the front door, where Todd's mother met us. She was holding the scraps for Rose in one hand, venison stew in the other. "Todd likes it," she said. "Will you eat it, do you think?"

Side by side, Todd's parents stood next to the car and spoke to me through the window. They were Todd's height and both wore navy windbreakers and brown glasses. They could be my parents, if I wanted.

All I had to do was reach out, scoop them up, nestle them in with the hay.

"I'll probably try it. Sure," I said. I rolled up the window and started backing down the long driveway. "She won't eat it if she don't like it," Todd's father shouted. "She's not stupid."

It was starting to get dark and I fumbled around until I found the headlights. In the distance, all I could see were sky and trees. Here you could see the sunset. You could see fall come and go. You could smell fall. You spoke of the horizon, not the skyline.

I had left a note for Todd telling him I'd be back around five. It was six now and he was probably starting to worry, probably wondering if I'd left him and taken the dog.

Todd looked out the kitchen window and waved when we pulled into the driveway. He had made a path through the house; lights were on in the kitchen, living room, bedroom.

Rose ran ahead of me and stood by the door. I left the venison in the car and scooped up an armful of hay. I wanted to walk in the door holding a bountiful bouquet. I wanted Todd to see who I was trying to become. A harvester.

He came to the door before I was there, and he and Rose stood looking at me coming down the walk. He was wearing the gray T-shirt with the holes. I was wearing hay. It was falling from my arms. Hay was strewn high and abundant around my feet like a bumper crop and there was only one thing I could think to say. "Here!"

The New Frontier

IT WAS MIM WHO made the wreath records, who melted the record albums, fluted their edges like a pie, and let Joel decorate them with dried quaking grass and roses; Mim who draped couch cover remnants over his shoulder to fashion him into King Ahasuerus for the Purim pageant; Mim who washed his hair while together they sang, "I'm gonna wash that dirt right out of my hair, gonna wash that dirt right out of my hair, gonna wash that dirt right out of my hair and send it on its way." But their lives changed, as did the lyrics. She changed the words back to Mary Martin's true feelings: "I'm gonna wash that *man* right out of my hair...and send him on his way." Joel thought Mim was washing the man out of his hair because he was growing up. He had just turned seven and maybe Mim thought he had been better when he was six, or five. There seemed to be some truth to this, for shortly after his birthday, she found, in the soapy crown of his head, a man she wanted out. And shortly after that she left. It wasn't till sometime later that he understood that the man in his hair was his father. That the dirt in his hair had died, then rose in the form of his father. That it was his father who had thrown out her old records, and the dried flowers, and the wooden rack in which the flowers hung, waiting to be sprayed gold and woven around the crimped edges of Burl Ives, Danny Kaye, Puccini.

Mim left differently than his real mother. She left with three neatly labeled cartons, two well-packed suitcases, a clothesline of dresses strung above the Buick's back seat, and visiting rights. Joel stayed with her four full months when his father was on the lecture circuit, nearly every weekend when his father was home.

Joel's real mother, as Mim told the story, left with the diary, a handbag, a hatbox, and enough money to get her back to Sioux City. She was tired—as Mim told it—of being a kind of lecture sea wife, waiting for his father to return from tours of *Rubber, Labor, and the American Corporation.*

She joined him on the road for a while, but that became hard for her, too, especially after Joel came along. She was twenty-one, homesick for her family and friends, heartsick for men who would pay attention to her, who would talk to her in tones not intended to reach the back row of a company classroom. She finally left Joel and his father during the windup of the Saginaw tour, but not before she had poured water over the Olivetti, layered black tape over the lecture notes. "If you loved me," she had said to his father, "you'd teach civics. You'd try harder to be normal." So that, Mim said, was that.

Soon after, while his father was home in Westville, he met Mim. She was an assistant to a local dermatologist, and on her lunch hour went to the Sterling Library to read *National Geographic.* He was compiling his notes for what was to become the Sputnik of his career. *Rubber and Synthetics: The New Frontier.* They met in the periodical room and they married after knowing each other only three months. Five months later, he left her with Joel—"a terrific two-year-old"—and went off on the tire company circuit. And with that, Mim said, we were on our way. A year after their divorce, his father still couldn't find the words to explain Mim's departure. He tried, when Joel insisted, to explain what he could. "It had to do with truth, trust, and . . ."

"The American corporation?" Joel asked.

"No. Different ways of seeing the same thing." But Joel, eight then, couldn't get it. He could never get to the bottom of things, never solve the mystery. When he asked for a more thorough explanation, his father raised both hands in front of him, as if the answer was written on the complicated network of his palms. The gesture came to be part of a regular dialogue, and Joel came to think of his father's palms as a shield—thought of the lines on his palms as the family's seal.

"Just explain it," he pleaded with Mim, "so a kid can get it."

She had just put a record album into a large spaghetti pot filled with boiling water. This stove in her small apartment had suggested cooking times printed above the gas burners. Standing Rib . . . 60 minutes; Rolled Shoulder . . . 75 minutes. "Record Album," she'd say to Joel, to which she taught him to answer, "Three minutes . . . for the busy homemaker."

"I got tired of your father," she said. "But not *sick* and tired of him like your real mother." She looked at her watch to time the cooking process, then put on a pair of rubber gloves. "You know how tired you get after we imagine we're medieval magicians trying to solve court murders?" Yes, he said, watching her as she removed the record from the pot with a pair of tongs. She set it on the counter, on a cloth towel, and deftly lifted up the hot, malleable sides until there were four arcs folded over the record label, in this case Bing Crosby's *Sweet Leilani*. "Well, I got tired of imagining who he was imagining I was: the personnel lady in Detroit; the lady foreman in Seymour."

She set a spray of dried cream roses into the center and turned the record around slowly, seeing it from different angles. "Not that I didn't love him. But your father was a one-man traveling show. He gave the lecture. He answered the questions. And he loved any woman who crossed his path." She took off the rubber gloves and set them under an empty clay flowerpot on her windowsill. "He let no parade pass him by." She put her hands on the album to turn it again, but it was still hot and she jumped back in pain. "He left no stone unturned." She turned on the faucet and ran cold water over her hands. "He left not a smear of moss under his feet."

Joel didn't get it at first. But once he did, he began to understand many other things as well. It was like mastering the first language, which, in turn, led to the mastery of all others.

He understood Marilyn Fineberg, a woman his father brought home several times. He understood her to be a modern-day murderer posing as a socialite party girl—Grace Kelly smile with a wicked witch liver. The first time his father brought her home, Joel was at the kitchen table coloring shapes he had cut from black construction paper. He had spread before him cutouts of clouds, pigs, a wolf, an airplane. He was using pastel chalks. Yellows, lavenders, pinks. Marilyn's dress was pink. She smelled like pink punch, like concentrated Hi-C added to explosive Fizzies. "What are you doing?" she asked, sitting in a chair next to him. His father stood in front of the kitchen counter, cutting up vegetables for dinner. Joel said nothing and continued layering colors into his clouds. He tried to imagine she wasn't there, that she didn't have a pink elbow threatening his pastels. His father finally spoke for him. "Joel's an artist. He just completed a decorative project in which he put clay over jars—a mayonnaise jar, a Manischewitz bottle. What else? A maple syrup jar with the little handle on it. Then he stuck on— adhered, if you like—these colorful, actually vibrant, stones. The kind you find in fish tanks?"

"Oh, how lovely," Marilyn said, her thin body quivering like a feeble fish on land. "May I see them?"

Joel pretended she hadn't asked the question. He blended his colors together with a cotton ball and kept his head down. For the first time he noticed the Formica tabletop was patterned with tiny bolts of lightning.

"Joel," his father said, "holy shit." Joel looked up, alarmed, and saw his father had cut his finger with the bread knife he was using to cut carrots. "Marilyn asked you," he said, "if she could see them." He was talking into his cut finger as though it were a microphone.

"I gave them all away except one, and I don't have it here."

"Is that the truth?"

"Yes."

"Is it at school?" his father asked, wrapping the finger with a green dish towel.

"No."

"Well, I guess I'll never get to see it," Marilyn moaned, flicking back her hair in order to reveal the knives she had for earrings.

"Sorry," Joel said. "Unless . . ."

"Unless . . ." Marilyn and his father said together. They both looked at him as if he were emerging from an egg.

". . . Unless you walk over to my mother's apartment, knock on her door, and tell her who you are and what you want."

His father turned around, his face flushed, his index finger a green, elephantine pistol aimed at Joel. "Please leave the room, Joel. And I think you should have dinner by yourself."

"I think so, too, Dad," he said. He put his pastels back into the box, his perfectly ordered rainbow, and put the cutouts into a small carton decorated with gold-sprayed macaroni. "You know," he said, realizing he had a captive, horror-stricken audience. "The truth is a hard pill to get down."

Truth was his father's favorite theme. Rubber was a close second. His father had paid his way through NYU by working factory jobs in the Naugatuck Valley, where he grew up. His major source of income and early identity was with the U.S. Rubber Company. While working on his PhD in economics, he discovered he could make money lecturing to trade groups, colleges, and senior management on the financial prospects of synthetic rubber. He traveled to tire, footwear, and chemical plants. He read papers at the annual Akron Rubber Group. His thesis was to emerge from his lecture material, but what emerged instead was a successful business. And the business couldn't afford a long absence to write the dissertation. Not when he had a wife and a son to feed. So he never stopped lecturing, looking for new angles. He collected reams of notes, broadened his themes to include plastics, elastomers, foreign competition. "It's an interesting subject," Mim said, "for maybe ten minutes. But to make it your life's work? Not that I didn't love him. But when I had the chance, I should have married a dermatologist."

Joel was glad Marilyn Fineberg wasn't there the day he brought home his fifth-grade report card from Mrs. Etz. She had written a note under the section called *comments*: "Joel is unquestionably intelligent and sensitive beyond his years. I see, however, a recurring moroseness. I have talked to him about this, but perhaps we should all sit down and talk."

Joel walked into his father's study to have him read and sign the report. The room was dark except for the large screen of light in the corner. His father was watching films of his lectures and making notes. The venetian blinds were closed tight, and he was writing by the light of a small Tensor lamp. Joel stood quietly in the doorway and watched the big screen catch and flash his father's face in the dark room. This was no Wyatt Earp or Sky King. This was not Gary Cooper in *High Noon*, Yul Brynner in *The Magnificent Seven*. This was Aaron Weissman, acting out yet another episode of *New Frontiers in Rubber*.

"I should never have told an opening joke to that group," he said, when he noticed Joel. "I could tell by their expressions they were business only." Joel saw that one man had a hand cupped over his nose, as though he was making a goose call. "Always feel out your group," his father said. "Try to know a little something about them before you start." As always, he sat behind his desk, in his tan, fast swivel chair—the chair that easily rolled to the typewriter, to the file cabinet, and, with a strong push, over to the phone. When his father was at the library or on the road, Joel would take the chair into the hall, run as fast as he could, then stand on the seat and fly.

"Why does Mrs. Etz say this?" his father asked. He set the report card down on his desk.

"I get morose sometimes."

"Why?"

"I miss my first mother."

"You never knew her."

"But she is my mother."

"Mim is your mother."

"But she doesn't even live here. You don't let me keep any mother I get."

He didn't look at Joel, but rather leaned way back in the chair and shut his eyes. He ran the tips of his fingers across his beard, as though trying to file down his already manicured nails. "The truth is," he said, "your father lectures better than he loves."

Joel stood by his desk, hoping for an elaboration. But his father had opened his eyes and seemed more interested in looking up, trying to gain a better understanding of the dark ceiling. Joel had to tug on his sleeve to get his attention. "You better tell that to Mrs. Etz. It probably should go into my file."

Mim cradled a blue rubber-soled shoe in both her hands. She and Joel were downstairs in the U.S. Rubber shoe room, in the bins. This was where the seconds—the flawed U.S. Rubber footwear—were displayed in steel cubicles, each the size of a roomy doghouse. Upstairs they sold firsts.

"I need the right," Mim said. She held the blue shoe in one hand and began poking through the bin looking for the mate. Joel tried to help her by crawling into the size 7s and foraging through the mass of mismatched shoes.

"There's a lot of green. How about two greens?"

"My sundresses are blue," she said. "I have the left."

"Beige would go, I have two beiges here."

"Never mind, sweetie, it's okay." But even as she said this, she continued her search.

Joel had come here before and bought sneakers with a misplaced line of glue or a broken eyelet where the lace came through. This time he had picked out red U.S. Keds. On TV he had seen a boy actually fly wearing new sneakers. P. F. Flyers. He was nine now, and he knew commercials were stories where events happened, characters spoke, and promises were made just to sell something. Nevertheless, when he got home he was going to jump off his father's Skychief.

He walked down the concrete aisles trying to find Mim's matching shoe. The light was dim, and everything around him—the red and green basketball shoes, the white and blue flip-flops—was the color of a baked potato. He pretended his body was a divining rod that would lead him to the right place. He stood by certain bins to see if he was pulled toward them or could pick up some sign.

Halfway down one aisle he felt himself being tugged and he tried to make his body loose and pliant so he could follow the lead. He closed his eyes and extended one arm ahead of him to pick up any strong signals that might come his way. But nothing came, and after a while he knew the game was over.

When he opened his eyes he was facing into a screened-off portion of the basement where rows of shopping carts overflowed with U.S. Keds. Lots of kids would be flying now. Kids would be jumping off house roofs and tall tree limbs. He'd pass kids in the air. The sky would become a kids' highway. High above Westville, waving to the grown-ups below, he'd be driving a red Pontiac with white laces.

"Joel!" Mim's voice sounded close, but he couldn't see her. "Are you hiding, honey?" He crawled into a bin of men's black rubbers and heaped as many as he could on top of him. "Don't hide too long because it's three o'clock!" He put a pair of rubbers over his face, leaving a small space so he could see her when she came by. The smell of rubber was everywhere in the U.S. Rubber shoe room. But for Joel, actually in the bin, the smell of rubber was an intoxicating slap in the face. He tried to breathe quietly, and because the smell was so strong, he tried not to breathe at all, and then to breathe like a church mouse, and then like a toad. He tried to think of something, but the only thing he could think of was rubber. A lot of things seemed to come down to rubber.

Seemingly unrelated things were related by rubber: an elastic band, an eraser, a tennis shoe, a ball. Maybe rubber, like DNA, was a building block of life. Maybe his father had to divorce two mothers so he could travel and spread the word. Maybe rubber was important. And if that were so, the possibility was even there that his father was important.

Mim approached the bin and stared right at him. "I wonder where he is," she said. He held still and tried hard to blend in. "Too bad he's lost," Mim said. "I thought we'd work with acrylics and dried brush root this afternoon." A stock clerk came by just then with a shopping cart of winter boots. He asked if she needed help. "My son is lost somewhere in here," she said, nodding her head toward Joel.

The clerk looked right at Joel and said, "What does he look like?"

"A little like me," Joel said. He didn't feel like playing: he felt like getting the story straight.

He crawled out from the bin and stood facing the clerk, a young man wearing navy chinos and a navy shirt. On his shirt pocket, in red capital letters, were the words *U.S. Rubber.*

"Do you know my father, Aaron Weissman?"

"No. Do you know my father, Arthur Johnson?"

"No. My father lectures about rubber."

"Somebody actually lectures on rubber?"

"Yes."

"Does anybody actually listen?"

He winked at Joel, then started down the aisle with his cart. As he walked away, he began whistling a song from *Snow White*, the song of the worker dwarfs. "Whistle While You Work." Joel remembered a time when Mim was washing his hair and he had sung, "Whistle while you work. Hitler is a jerk." Mim stopped lathering his head and looked him straight in the eyes. "If you ever mention that name again," she said, "so help me. I'll slap you."

"The upper echelon listens," Mim said. The clerk moved down the aisle, whistling, pushing the cart. "Your top management and engineers need to hear what Mr. Weissman has to say." Her voice was on medium high, but he didn't answer. He lifted up the tongue on a pair of boots, looked for something, then threw the boots into a bin.

Mim grabbed Joel's hand and whispered, "Don't talk to him. I don't want to encourage rude behavior." They waited in line by the counter to pay for Joel's Keds. Joel, following Mim's lead, tried a combination of glowering and perfect silence. He pressed his lips together tightly and squinted his eyes. He pretended that if he spoke a word, he would be killed. And he entertained a thought that made him so sad he didn't want to talk, anyway: perhaps flight was impossible when wearing seconds.

Joel and Mim were sitting at her small kitchen table, painting dried wishbones. She had been saving them for a year, in a plastic bag, and on Saturday morning she showed them to Joel. "I don't know," she said, looking away from him. "But I always wanted to do something with these."

Her idea was to arrange them into a collage, but Joel had suggested making a mobile. In fact, he thought of demonstrating how to make a dried-bone mobile for the *How It's Done* speech he had to give to his class. The winner of the class contest competed against the whole school.

Mim said a bone mobile was in interesting idea for a speech but suggested he ask his father's opinion. "We have to grant him one undeniable thing," she said. "He is, if nothing else, a brilliant lecturer."

"Rubberneck?"

"Rubberneck."

"He just got back from Akron. And he's too in love with Roberta Kugel."

"Give him a chance." Joel actually liked it when Mim gave his father special consideration or brought him into their conversations. He didn't like to think that he had to deal with his father by himself; that as an only child, he was the only accomplice to a suave, well-spoken geek.

"What is Roberta like?" Mim asked.

"Besides having a nose like a B-52?"

"Really?"

"And she uses too much hair spray."

"How much?"

"She sprays her head for only about ten minutes in the downstairs bathroom. And after she's finished, you can't light a match if she's in the same room."

"Are you lighting matches again?"

"And she doesn't know the recipe for Three Beans Mim."

"She wouldn't, honey, because I made that up."

"And she stinks."

"She has an odor?"

"Of cigarette smoke."

"No."

"Between her lipstick smeared on her chin and her stale breath, my father will never be able to kiss her. Who could?"

"That's probably enough, Joel. I suppose we should say something good about her."

"She does have nice blond hair on her forearms."

"There you go."

Aaron thought Joel's speech should be "How to Test for Worn Tires."

Even Roberta, whom his father had known just one week, thought the idea was ill-advised. "He's only ten," she said. "He doesn't drive, and he shouldn't have to care about that stuff. I've never cared about worn tires."

"You just have to care about looking beautiful," Aaron said, patting her hand.

"And I just have to care about not being boring," Joel said.

"But if you make it to the finals you'll be speaking to parents. And parents need to know about worn tires. Audience. Always consider your audience."

Joel looked at Roberta's face and knew she wouldn't be around next week.

"You can put three tires side by side, each showing a different wear pattern. One with wear bars across the tread, one with spotty wear, and one with a flat spot." He paused and put a lanky arm over Roberta. "You can identify the wear pattern and then offer a solution. Like having the tires balanced if you have spotty wear, or changing your braking technique if you have a bald spot."

"Honey," Roberta said, rubbing his father's high, pale forehead, "I think you better change your technique."

"They'll laugh at me," Joel said.

"Listen to this," his father said. He paused while he put his free hand into his pants pocket and brought out some loose change. He placed the dimes and nickels on the coffee table and held onto a penny. Removing his arm from Roberta's shoulder, he held the coin in one hand and pointed to it with the other. Joel and Roberta stared at him. Harry Houdini ready to make magic.

"Okay, now. Look. Stick a penny into the tire groove, head first. If you can see the top of Lincoln's head above the tread rubber, the tire is bald."

Roberta looked at Joel and rolled her eyes.

Joel imagined for one painful moment that he was Roberta. He saw deep lines in his father's neck. Round, small spots on his cheek which matched the brown of his glasses. And he saw that the eyes behind the glasses were eager and wide, like he was begging the teacher to call on him, without raising his hand.

Joel went to his room and thought about what interested him. He spoke to his real mother, something which helped him to calm down or analyze a situation. Hers was a reasonable voice that told him not to jump off cars or be rude to his father's girlfriends.

"Dear, Mom," he began. "Help me to know what is right." He adapted his approach from a spiritual show he saw on TV and from the children's service conducted by his rabbi. "Show me the way of the shepherd and let me be better than anybody else."

Imagine yourself, she said, in a cloud. You're high in the sky, floating,

floating, higher than everyone, halfway to God. Look down. What do you see?

Mrs. Etz called his speech "imaginative, concise, thoroughly researched, and rigorously organized." His classmates called his speech "not boring" and unanimously elected him to speak in the schoolwide *How It's Done* contest. Neither Mim nor his father knew what his subject was. He invited them to the finals, glad that Roberta was out of the picture and his parents would be there together.

The contest was held in the evening, and the school in the dark was big and remote, beyond reach, its high windows and brick sides looking more like U.S. Rubber than Sheridan School. It was March, and the trees were still frozen, their branches like black wishbones clenching the edge of the parking lot.

There were twelve finalists, who littered the stage with soap powder, potting soil, glitter, paper scraps, and flour. Being a Weissman, he was last. Sandra Valiante had come right before him with her speech, "How to Grow Luscious Fruit." The back of the auditorium looked like a yard sale, with long library tables piled high with props. Draped across the back of the stage was a handwritten banner: HOW TO . . . 1962.

The judges sat in the first row of the parents' aisle. One judge, the science teacher, had taken his glasses off and was rubbing his eyes hard as though he never planned to see again. Another judge was yawning, and one judge, wearing a knit pullover, devoted her remaining energy to pulling loose lint from her dolman sleeves.

People in the audience were coughing a lot by now and shifting in their seats. Even the principal walked over to the judges and tapped his watch. He then walked onto the stage and introduced Joel.

Joel floated above the audience. He looked down at the parents, the kids, the teachers. He saw their arms wrapped around their chests as though trying to keep the wind out. High above them all, floating in place, he had a thought that was entirely new and altogether startling—a thought that, for a second, took his breath away. The speaker can see the audience. He could see the blues and reds, shirts and ties, jackets, pearls. The audience was not, as he had always considered, invisible. The audience could not, as he used to believe, talk, sleep, chew, pick—and expect to get away with it. He could see them all. And they could see him. But it didn't matter. Standing on stage was like finding Akron on the globe and knowing that in the scheme of the big ball, Akron didn't matter.

"Well, it's been a long evening. And I can tell that some of you are having trouble sitting still. Now you know how we all feel by the end of a school day." The audience laughed a little, a low groan that sounded like furniture dragged across linoleum.

"I'm going to ask you to imagine something right now. It will be easier if you close your eyes." He paused. "Good. Now you even *look* like us at the end of the day." The audience laughed a little louder. "Okay, now please close your eyes."

He looked into the audience and spotted Mim and his father. Mim sat beside him with her eyes shut tight. His father had his eyes wide open and clapped his hands silently in the air, applauding Joel.

"I want you to make believe you live in Iowa, and not Connecticut. And I want you to imagine it's been dark and windy all day, and now you're listening to the radio. All of a sudden the announcer has interrupted the song to say a tornado is coming, and you better be ready. That's the background. The topic of my speech is . . ." He had an easel set up on the stage with a huge pad of paper. He ripped off the first sheet and uncovered the large, handwritten title: "How to Survive a Tornado." He turned on a tape recorder and played a recording of static-y silence, followed by hailstones (he had to stop the tape and say to the audience, "hailstones"). He tore the title page off the pad, and behind it was a picture he'd drawn of a cloud bulging downward, forming a funnel.

"If you hear and see this, you'll wish you had a specially designed tornado shelter. Anyone who has seen or been in an air raid shelter already has an idea of what this is like." A third-grader, a neighbor of Joel's who sat three rows from the front, called out in a voice so small and timid it took Joel a few seconds for the sentence to register. "Can we open our eyes now?" Joel looked at him, his head down and his arms wrapped across his face as though waiting for the bombs to drop. "Only if you want, Benny."

His only other props were a diagram he had drawn, which showed the shape and dimensions of a shelter, and a large shopping bag, which he kept visibly in front of the podium. He used a pointer. He walked easily from the diagram to the podium and back to the diagram. He spoke slowly and used expressions like *notice, if you will*; *now, let's assume*; *can people in the back row see?*

He concluded by asking, "Now that you've built your shelter, what do you put in it? Anybody want to guess?"

"Something to wet your whistle," a man shouted. "Water or soda."

"Okay," Joel said. "Anything else?"

"Canned soup. Beef in a can."

"Right," Joel said, walking over to the shopping bag and pulling out a can of Campbell's soup. He set it on the podium. "What else?"

"Your homework," a kid yelled.

"Nice try," Joel said. He looked down at the audience, his audience: the reds, the blues, the tangerines, taking turns standing up, waving their hands.

"Yes," Joel said. "The gentleman in the back row."

"A flashlight," the man said.

"Very good, sir," Joel said, pulling a flashlight out of the bag and setting it on the podium. "Who else wants to take a guess?"

"A radio," called out a classmate of Joel's who had already heard the speech and knew the answers.

"You're all doing much better than the kids in my class," Joel said, looking at him.

"What else? What if your flashlight and radio go out on you?"

A woman screamed out. "Batteries!"

"Right," Joel said. "And I see I'm running out of time, so I'll show you what other essentials I have in my bag." He pulled out—one at a time for dramatic effect—a stuffed rabbit, a Boy Scout canteen, and a copy of *Mad* magazine, Alfred E. Neuman wearing a pirate's hat and a patch over his eye.

"Any questions?" Many people raised their hands, and he wasn't sure whom to call on first. The science teacher had his hand up and so did the woman who taught art. Benny was standing up, waving his hand as though flagging down a low-flying airplane. The principal walked on stage just then, a signal that the event was over. But someone called out a question, anyway. "How many people can you comfortably take with you into your shelter?"

It took Joel a second to find the voice. It was his father.

The principal was by his side now and answered for him.

"Time, Mr. Weissman. Time, everyone. Sorry, but the judges need their time, too. And so do John Letts and his clean-up crew." Joel looked down at his father. His legs were crossed. Those impossibly long legs. Drum major legs that when crossed, like now, forced his knees high into the air, nearly hiding his chin and mouth. He signaled to the principal—a slow, formal military salute.

It wasn't the smooth ending Joel had imagined, so he just held the rabbit over his head and said, "That's it. Thank you for being such a great audience."

In the car on the way home his father said it took brains and guts to give a speech like that. Mim was sitting on the passenger side in the front seat and she turned to look at Joel, who had his arm draped around a large box, a set of *World Book Encyclopedia*. "I learned something from your speech. And it had nothing to do with tornadoes."

"That he's his father's son?" his father said.

"I wouldn't take it that far."

Joel left the car and floated above it. He gave all his attention to the night, to the long dark streets, houses with lights on in every room, people passing by windows, people wearing nightgowns, brushing their hair, holding plates, looking like they belonged exactly where they were.

Sweethearts

IF I AM AN ORANGE, Sam is an orange.

If I am half an orange, Sam is the other half.

He may or may not be the better half, but he's certainly *the other*.

I can count the ways we got here: one fiberglass tub installation, two top-loading washers, four sets of flannel sheets, two kids, two upright vacuum cleaners, two tall kitchen stools, seven asbestos-covered basement pipes, eight million backyard cockroaches in Baltimore, six years in Belltown, four years on Fells Avenue. I should mention twelve years of love. I'm blushing.

Sam greets me now at the front door. He's wearing another stupid baseball hat: *Auto Parts for Auto People*. It's night and the porch is dark, but behind Sam the living room is ablaze with light and bright toy debris. "How was the meeting?" he asks.

"Auto Parts for Auto People?" I say.

"What?"

"Your hat. Where'd you get that?"

He takes it off and looks at it. "Beats me," he says and puts it back on.

Telling him his hats are stupid would be the same as telling him his eyes are too blue. Which they are. But they come with the orange. Buy the orange, buy the pith.

"How was the meeting?" he asks again, and I turn my head away. I can't believe he didn't pick up any toys.

"You're not an auto person," I say.

"What?"

"Your hat. Are you an Auto People?"

He shrugs. If it's a hat, he wears it. Life is so simple for him.

"The meeting was okay," I say as we walk into the living room. With my foot, I push aside a crowd scene of wooden dolls with yarn hair. "But Sandy Wargo hates me."

"Why?"

"No reason. I just exist in her neighborhood."

"You exist in hers."

"But she was here first. And she's hateful."

"You're smarter and cuter," he says, and I'm halfway in love again. At that moment, in his hat, he looks like a man, a father, not concerned with looks or pretense. A decent guy who happens to collect stupid hats. But then there's his orange long-sleeve T-shirt: *5-K Pumpkin Race.*

"No, really," he says. "Why does she hate you?"

"I'm a stranger in these parts," I say and stop there. I don't want to press the point that we made a mistake buying this big colonial in the North End. Didn't we know I'd get pregnant and have to send our kids to Commodore Peasley School? Where the PTA is an excuse for mothers to congregate monthly in the library and hate me?

Now hate is a big word but Sandy Wargo is big. Big in the hip, wide in the mouth. At one point in tonight's meeting, when the PTA treasurer was searching for a report and the library was stone silent, Sandy turned to the secretary and said, "About Marissa? I didn't hurt her. I just stunned her."

Now I don't know Marissa. She wasn't at the PTA meeting and I should know since I'm president. And I don't know exactly what *stun* means to Sandy Wargo. To me it means, *I didn't kill Marissa; I just grazed her neck with my stun gun.*

I might be president but I scare easily. Were my children safe in this school? But the meeting went on, and the principal, since I was new at leadership, directed our attention to the issue of fundraising. And here's where Sandy took off.

"All's I know is we have just enough money to send the second grade to the apple orchard. Other than that, squat." I looked at her breasts. They looked less mean than her face but not totally benign. For my baby, my breasts are food and beverage, a place to rest, to hang her hat. Sandy's breasts are poison apples: big, with a long, dark stem of cleavage rising above a yellow sweater.

The treasurer supported her. "Sandy's right. We have $238.49. Other PTAs in town have at least three thousand dollars. Spencer School has so much money they take out high-earning CDs."

"Candy sells and candy's easy," Sandy went on. She has red hair, big eyes, pillowy cheeks. Dimples. Mean people are often cute. They can misbehave and redeem themselves with their dimples. "Besides which," she said, "you got December and January. You got Valentine's Day. Right here you got three excellent candy months. We always sell candy and candy works for us." Her husband, a big man himself, sat by her side and nodded.

My face burned as I prepared to talk. I imagined my ears looked like something you'd find in a salad: red and fluted. "What about mugs or wrapping paper?" Once full and clear, my voice has become thin and flat from dealing with children, loneliness, laundry. "The town leagues, the scouts, are all doing candy," I said. "I'm wondering if candy gives kids the message that candy is the only thing there is."

"We go through this c-r-a-p every year," Sandy said. "We always come back to candy." I saw her breasts rise and fall, rise and fall. They were talking for her: she the surly puppeteer, the expressive breasts her puppets.

"What about an auction?" I asked.

"Look at us," she said. "We gonna do an auction?"

I looked around at the six of us scattered about the ten, round library tables. Sandy was right. We didn't look like we could do an auction. We didn't look like we could make it home.

"We're outta here," Sandy said all of a sudden. She prepared to stand, putting a hand on her husband's leg to help her out of the chair. She'd been president for three years and didn't want to do it anymore. So the principal suggested me, and I suggested I was unfit for the position. "We have no one," she said, which made me feel fitter. If no one could do it, so could I.

To his credit, Sandy's husband comes to all the meetings with her. Also to his credit, he always looks scared. "We're going home to give our kids candy," she said. "That's the message we give our kids. Candy is good. It's better than booze or drugs." Her breasts, rising and falling, were downright eloquent.

But I don't say this to Sam. I try to keep things upbeat. "I think she might, at some point, try to kill me."

"Why did you agree to be president?" he asks. "The meetings just upset you." He pushes his baseball cap to the back of this head until his forehead, his receding hairline, is a vast expanse of field and sky.

I walk past him, into the dining room. "It's a night out."

In the kitchen, I see the result of my day. Dishes and mugs stacked like Lincoln logs, as high as Lincoln's Tennessee home. We have a dishwasher, but someone has to load it. Meanwhile, Lincoln is alive and trapped inside, pinned against a pine chifferobe. I was hoping when I was at the meeting, Sam would have freed him. Free Lincoln! But Sam's not a dish man.

I'd like to give him a break. He bathed the girls, read them a book, put them to bed. All this after a day at work. Still, I make a mental note that in the future I should ask Sam, point blank, with no moral finger pointing, if he can do just a few dishes. But at the moment I can't say it. Instead, I point the finger at myself. "I don't care if Sandy Wargo hates me. That's her problem. But I know my hair was sticking up behind my ears the whole meeting and she's unforgiving. One episode of my hair sticking up and she'll always tell people, 'Her hair sticks up.'"

"Wear a hat," he says.

"The real issue is I'm an oddball at Peasley School. I speak when not spoken to. I wear clogs."

"Face it, Sunny. We'd be oddballs anywhere."

He knows about odd. Before Jayney was born, he was the youngest member of the Belltown Symphonic Band, where he played with local, much older merchants, barbers, optometrists. At rehearsals, the old gents would wear dress pants and acrylic vests while Sam wore wrinkled work shirts and worn corduroy pants that made his skinny legs look like the thin brass of his trombone.

"We wouldn't be odd everywhere," I say.

"I would. Put me anywhere and I'd be odd. Just join me." He puts out his hand.

"No," I say, taking offense. "I know there are places I wouldn't be odd."

Something, an itch, prompts him to take off his hat. I see that thin wisps of his black curly hair have left the pack and are going off on their own. The curls covering his forehead keep rising higher and higher like the tide. Eventually, while I'm not looking, the curls will recede to the crown, then down, then topple backward.

"Did Rae go down easy at bedtime?" I ask.

"I gave her a bottle of Ninnie and she went down like a dream." He goes into the kitchen looking for something to eat himself. He stands before the dirty dishes as if they don't exist. To him, they don't. "You're lucky you can stay home with her!" he calls to me. "Are there any snacks?"

"I keep telling you to grow breasts, Sam. Grow Ninnies, then you can stay home and lift your shirt all day."

"I'd lift my shirt," he says. "Boy, would I lift my shirt. My meat man just left and Stop & Shop just bought out Edwards. I don't know what's what right now. I'd give anything to bag it and stay at home. You can't get a good meat man!"

"That's for sure."

"What?"

"Are you sure?"

"I'm looking. The right man is out there somewhere."

"Grow breasts," I say, "and I'll cut the meat."

"Watch your language," he says.

The next evening Sam comes home at eight. Rae has fallen asleep on the living room rug, her little face pressed against floor lint. Jayne, in her pink pajamas, runs to give him a hug. I can't bear to look at him. I have done everything an average of twelve times before he's gotten home. I have nursed Rae eleven times; served a combination of nine snacks and meals; poured ten servings of diluted juice; cleaned the kitchen eleven times; folded thirty-two pieces of laundry; answered nine phone calls; asked Jayne ten times to pick up her socks and yelled about it five times; stooped down nineteen times to pick up bits of string, juice straws, magazine subscription cards, plastic pets, marker tops, glueless stickers, blanket threads, wet panties, moist tights, perforated paper strips, pennies, and a feather.

When Sam walks in, I am standing in front of the kitchen sink. My hips sway, and I can feel the dance coming on, the Quickstep.

"You should have called if you were going to be so late."

"You're right."

"My life is a million baby steps that lead nowhere," I say.

"You'll never guess who I saw today."

I turn around from the sink, but I don't look at him. I direct my eyes to the floor where I see either a drop of hot chocolate or a spot of blood.

"Please guess who I saw."

"Did you hear what I said?"

"Yes, I'm sorry. I'll call next time. Will you guess?"

"Did you hear the part about my life?"

"I heard. I know. I'm sorry about the million steps. But just play with me, okay? Guess who I saw?"

"You met your meat man."

"No. Vivian Comacho."

"Who's that?"

"You don't remember me talking about her?"

"Just tell me, okay? I don't know her."

"Vivian Comacho was Beth Sabo's best friend in college."

Now Beth Sabo was a name I knew. Beth Sabo was Sam's first long-term, coming-of-age, always-thought-of-with-ardent-wistfulness girl-friend. Vivian Comacho, however, meant nothing to me.

"Vivian Comacho was a run-around in college," he says. "Flirty and flighty. She was really hard to figure out. Went from guy to guy. She was heavy then, but she looks great now. Still pretty, but slimmer. She kept saying things like, 'My partner went to Morocco; my partner changed law firms; my partner and I made a wicked beef and pork chili.'"

"Yes?" I say.

"So, lesbian," he says.

"Yes?" I say pointedly conveying that this is not at all surprising to me, since I never knew the woman and can't feel much of anything. But I think he knows me well enough to know that the life of lesbians *is* a life I think about. I like their road; I'd choose their road as long as I could live with women, have sex with men.

"Good for her," I say.

"That's what I say. I always said women are nicer than men."

"That's for sure."

"I'm not late every night."

"Every single night."

"Only since the meat man left."

"Isn't there a butcher clearing house?"

"I'm particular. If I can't find someone I like, I'll keep doing it myself."

It amazes me he can be sloppy at home; so neat about meat.

"So, we made a date to meet at O'Rourke's," he says. "This Saturday. To catch up. We'll meet real early, then I'll come home."

"I never get to go to O'Rourke's," I say. Being around little girls makes you talk and think like them.

"I'll take you sometime."

Jayne calls out from the living room. "I want to go to O'Rourke's, too. I want to have pancakes."

"I'll take both of you to O'Rourke's sometime. Rae, too."

"Right," I say. "I'll start the girls' bath."

"Are you going on a date, Daddy?" Jayne calls out. She has laid all her dolls on top of the radiator and is now covering them with sheets of toilet paper. This is how she puts them to bed.

"Not really," he says. "Mommy's my date. My wife. This person is an old friend."

"She's lesbian?"

"Yes."

"What's that?"

"A woman who would rather date another woman than a man."

"Why she going out with you?"

"That's my question," I say, as I head upstairs to the bathroom.

In our house, the bathroom like all the other rooms is solid plaster, with a solid wood door behind which you can really barricade yourself. I turn on the faucet, then sit down on a thick towel and lean against the fiberglass tub. The force of the water sends hard blows to my back. I close my eyes and see myself back at Aetna where I'm commandeering a long wooden conference table that, with a hearty rudder, could sail clear to Norway. While I'm steering the table, I advise a group of product managers to offer more investment options to retirees. *Offer them a simplified asset management account*, I tell them, which is what I told them in real life. Real life before Jayney.

The scene changes: I am now in a nun's habit, my head bowed, my teeth unclenched. Dear Lord, I begin, but then I run out of words. This is because I'm not a nun. I'm a mother stealing a few moments peace. A thief in a dirty sweatshirt.

· · ·

The next morning, I try unsuccessfully to convince Jayne to buy a few of the school's hot lunches for the week. It would be a few less lunches I'd have to make. But she won't agree. She says if she signs up for a taco they substitute hot dogs. If she signs up for macaroni and cheese, they substitute hamburgers. She's right and I can't blame her. At the bottom of the weekly printed lunch menu, I see a disclaimer: *Subject to substitutions.*

"Okay," I say. "I'll make you lunches this week but next week you'll make your own." She is busy examining a patch of clear and perfect skin under yet another Band-Aid. Band-Aids go on my shopping list every week, along with bread and milk. She often checks the status of her arms and legs, always looking for a small sign of purple or red which might suggest some injustice to her skin.

"You hear me, Miss Wound Checker? I can't do it all. Next week you'll make your own lunch. For crying out loud."

I have pretty much guaranteed that she will never want to make her own lunch; that she will be forever joyless about making her lunch; that she will develop such a distaste for making her own lunch that she will pull from the freezer a frozen dinner and take that to school. At Commodore Peasley, in her blue plaid dress, she will be known as the little girl who sucks on frozen Crab Rangoon.

She is a beautiful girl. Brown hair, brown eyes, fair skin with a wash of rose on her cheeks. I am a fretful witch lugging around my wickedness with loathing and regret.

I make her lunch, make hot oatmeal for breakfast, give Rae her wake-up Ninnie, get Jayne and Rae dressed, tie their shoes, get them in the car, drive Jayne to school. Then it's home to more Ninnie for Rae, who knocks on my breasts as if they're a door. If I tell her Ninnie is busy or Ninnie is tired she knocks harder.

I had planned to be behind this by now. Once Jayne started first grade, I'd planned to go back to my job. But I got pregnant and here I am all over again. Ninnie in the morning, Ninnie in the evening,

Ninnie at suppertime. Be my little Ninnie and love me all the time. I could put Rae in day care and go back to work, but there's the cost. And the Ninnie factor. Who'd believe a thirteen-month-old needs so much Ninnie. She should be beyond Ninnie by now. She should be more fond of solid food: a little sweet potato, a little hunk of banana, a sliver of flank steak. But she wants me.

Your last child, I tell myself. Your last chance to do it right. I myself didn't have Ninnie. I had a bottle with formula and a family whose bodies were locked inside their heads. They double-locked the bathroom door even when they were washing their hands or looking for a cotton ball.

I put Rae on my back and we walk to the gym. As we enter the shopping plaza, I see Sandy Wargo pulling into Waldbaum's. She's driving a black Camaro, and her hair is voluminous and red. I can barely see her face in profile through the thick hair. I wave my arm high as though we are old buddies from back when, and by chance have run into each other. I consider yelling, "Sandy!" But then ask myself why. I don't even like her.

She doesn't return my wave, anyway. She either sees me or doesn't see me. Who's to know?

World Gym, in the corner of the plaza, is only a few blocks from my house and offers two hours of babysitting in the morning. I am so grateful to pass Rae over to Stephanie, the babysitter, who looks lovingly at Rae and says, "How's the Poopmeister?" She takes Rae and snuggles with her cheek to cheek.

Stephanie has a bountiful bouquet of yellow roses on a chair near the TV.

"Beautiful roses," I say. "Two dozen?"

"Twenty-two. I love yellow."

"Yellow is a good color for you," I say. "Against your dark hair." She is a pretty girl, around nineteen, who wears her hair in a high ponytail. I used to wear my hair in a ponytail but then cut it short, thinking short looked more sophisticated with my dirty sweatshirts. "From an admirer?" I ask.

"From my friend, Tom. At Howard's Discounts."

Rae starts to fuss in her arms and I leave before the fussing turns to body-belting screams that accompany our separation.

I'm about to get on the treadmill when Austin, a gym regular, starts walking in my direction. I've noticed him for the past three months. He's easy to notice. He's somewhere between sixty and seventy, short and bullish. For a gym bag, he carries a large leather satchel, shaped like a tool box. When he's assisting a man power lift, he makes a huge, sexual shout of exertion and hollers: "Yes, yes, yes, good, good, good man, you got it, yes, yes, go, go, come to me, baby. Nice job." He's the old guy yelling and I'm the mother on the treadmill. I figure everyone sees him and no one sees me. He proves me wrong.

"It's 1868," he says, for an opener. "And you and I are on the Oregon Trail from St. Louis to the Willamette Valley."

"Me?"

"You are driving the wagon. I have chosen you because I need a pioneer woman and that's you. I get shot and you bandage me. You don't leave me just because I can't carry my weight."

Which is considerable. "Strong and cute," he later describes himself, while he's in between sets and I'm ten minutes into the treadmill. He shows me a black-and-white backlit photo of him posing on a UPS carton. "I was national champion," he tells me. "And you're a pioneer woman. No frills. Just a good, healthy specimen."

"Austin at the gym came onto me," I say to Sam that night. "He told me I could drive his pioneer wagon."

"Sounds sexual to me," Sam said. "Who is this guy?"

"I think I'll ask him to O'Rourke's," I say.

"That's tomorrow morning, remember," he says to me. "Vivian and I will meet at O'Rourke's, then I'll bring her back here to meet you."

"So, I stay here and do the usual and you have apple pancakes with someone who is your old girlfriend's old friend."

"She's a lesbian."

"Not this again," I say.

"I'll take the girls in the afternoon," he says. "I'll take them some-where. You can do whatever you want."

"I want breakfast pancakes, at O'Rourke's," I say.

He takes off his basketball hat, scratches his head, closes his eyes.

Somehow breakfast with Vivian becomes, in my mind, breakfast sex. I reason it's the fact that Vivian is associated with the girl Sam first had sex with.

It's not like I really want to have "breakfast" with Sam. Rae drains Ninnie dry; Jayne tests my will; Lincoln, from beneath the pile of dishes, calls out to be liberated. They all put my brain and body in a bad mood.

And I'm in a terrible mood the next morning when at seven, the sky still dark, Mr. Early Bird, expectant and exuberant, leaves for O'Rourke's. "Where's your stupid hat?" I say, before he sets off.

"I can't find it."

"I'll find it for you."

"I'm running late."

I do all the girl care and house care, and he returns at ten fifty. He doesn't just return, however. He knocks on the front door, as if he's a guest, and when we go to answer, there she is: cooler than a cucumber, cuter than a fresh water pearl—Vivian Comacho. Maybe it's Coman-cho. Sam has a tendency to slur his speech when he gets excited. I'd get excited around her too. She throws off deep puffs of cool air as she stands on the porch with her cropped leather jacket and charcoal sweats. Her shiny, succulent pony tail is pulled puckishly through the back hole in her green, wool baseball hat. She is taller than I, a good five feet seven, her sweats are clean, and with her even, white teeth she is a picture of a lanky, perky, oh-so-casual Saturday date.

"She's a lesbian," Jayne explains to Rae, who is crouched behind us, examining some floor lint. I'm hoping the cold air, the wind, will prevent Vivian from hearing this.

Jayne is wearing a pink-and-purple flannel dress with patterned tights and patent shoes with a big bow. Vivian looks down at her and says, "Are you going to the ball?"

Jayne hides behind me and says, "There's no such thing as balls. Only dress-up and weddings."

"Is this dress-up?"

"Yes. No one's getting married today."

"Smart girl," Vivian says, and she puts her hand out to me. "I'm Vivian."

I don't shake. I'm mad and one of my eyes is swollen from house dust. I'm wearing a long, lilac-colored shirt that, I notice now, has a perfectly round coffee cup ring on the hem. The ring can only mean that someone, without thinking, must have set a cup of coffee down on my shirt. With me in it.

In contrast to me, the house looks good. It looks good and presentable. I have worked to present a look, a lie, of cleanliness, beauty, well-being. Another switch in my life has occurred where, when company comes, I am more concerned with dressing and cleaning the house than myself. If I am the tortoise, the house is my shell, the part I show. The house has become me and I have become its handmaiden.

"Hi," I say to her and back off. I let my house speak for itself. So, here it is. I skulk away like the embarrassed scullery maid caught fraternizing with the court's exalted High Lesbian.

Sam takes a good look at me and says, "Why don't we just take the girls for a walk and you can have some free time." *We* is he and Vivian, who have become, if not a couple, at least a twosome—paired off and joined together by college, pancakes, and now my children.

"It's a beautiful fall day," Vivian says. "Sam and I have already walked around Eastern Valley Hospital, where I used to work. I could walk all day." Fresh air is pouring from her mouth, and her cheeks have the red imprint of a flowering primrose. "My only Saturday chore is to buy a hair dryer."

"My smallest chore," I say, "is to fold five baskets of laundry." But saying this gives me no edge because we're playing different games.

"Let's get the girls ready," Sam says, and he and Vivian come in the front door. I run to find the girls' coats and the back carrier for Rae.

I find Rae's coat but not Jayne's. I am upstairs, partly looking, partly hiding.

"I found something!" Vivian calls out. "A purple thing."

What she has found, in the back closet, a place she shouldn't have been, is a sweater of mine. It is a small sweater, maybe a little too short, but it is still a grown-up sweater. I don't say anything, and Sam says, "That's fine."

I peer from the top of the steps and see them all leaving from the front door. Rae is in her back carrier on Sam's back. Vivian puts her hand out for Jayne, but Jayne doesn't take it. Jayne, my big girl, is also a Ninnie graduate and a serious reader and I know she has read me. She actually walks down the porch steps with her elbows bent and her hands spread before her. This is her impression of a surgeon who has scrubbed and shuns anything that is not certifiably sterile.

Folding clothes is as quiet as it is useless. Sam's T-shirts, Rae's rompers, Jayne's leggings are all soundlessly rapt, limp and soft in my hand. They are like the children of my children.

I have folded and refolded each piece here so many times that I've become a cotton onesie. I am Sam's T-shirt.

I need something to keep going. A Mars bar. I am desperate for one. I start looking all over the house for old Halloween candy. All I find is an ancient caramel Nips, ragged and rough. I have to suck hard to get any taste at all. I keep sucking until some flavor, no longer caramel, comes out. And I keep sucking still, trying to decide if the candy is too stale or just a little stale and then I suck more trying to figure it all out until, before I know it, I have sucked and chewed the whole thing. The candy is gone and I haven't yet made up my mind. Did I like the candy or not? Was it okay? I wish I had another chance because stale or not, this is what I have—what was given to me.

Ninety minutes later, they come back, smiling from their walk with Vivian. "We walked all over Wesleyan and stopped at the observatory,"

Sam says. His face looks energized; his dark stubble is aglow. The girls have red, almost rashy cheeks and their hair is cool to the touch.

"Where's Vivian?"

"Kmart," he says. He sits down on the couch. "Did you have a nice time?"

"Folding clothes?"

"If that's how you chose to use your time." I head toward the kitchen where I'll sit on the floor and try to make my mind a blank. "What did you think of her?" he calls out to me. I don't answer and he comes into the kitchen to find me. He doesn't ask why I'm sitting on the floor; he just sits down beside me, as if this is where we happen to find ourselves. "So, what did you think?"

He asks this hopefully, a son asking his mother what she thinks of his betrothed.

"She's pretty. She looks happy, content, in charge of her life."

"Of course," he says, putting an arm around me and crushing me into the cabinets behind us. He whispers into my ear. "She doesn't have kids."

At his touch, my eyes get teary and my throat gets tight. I can barely talk but I must say this: "I love our kids."

"I know," he says, rubbing my back. "I know."

The next day, Sunday, Sam is on the phone with an old college friend. This is a friend he calls when he has many household chores and doesn't know where to start. He calls Al to help transport him from, say, eating cereal to wrapping asbestos pipes in the basement.

"Al!" he says, speaking on the kitchen phone. I have to clean the basement but wanted to give you a quick call. He listens, then says, "Okay, okay, good. Actually my meat man left and Stop & Shop is ready to take us over. But guess who I ran into?"

His face is flushed. "No, no, no. Vivian Comacho."

I look at him straight on and imagine he's an exacting ophthalmologist: I roll my eyes again three times.

"No, no, not that one. She was Beth's best friend at Bridgeport. She's lost at least sixty pounds. She's beautiful and she's a lesbian."

I stand at the sink and investigate a bad smell. It could be a smell from current bad food or a lingering, phantom smell from long ago. A piece of bad meat thrown away but smelling in perpetuity.

"She's a lawyer. Before that a nurse."

I run a lemon rind through the garbage disposal.

Sam lowers the receiver to his chin and hisses. "I'm on the phone." He puts the phone back to his ear and says, "Yeah. But she's different. Came into her own. She's blossomed."

"A flowering narcissus," I say. "A blooming cactus," I say even louder.

Sam lowers the phone again. "Sunny, if you can't control yourself, leave the room."

"Sunny," I say, "if you can't control yourself..."

But then Jayne screams from the living room. "Help! I lost my horse!"

Once again she has lost a miniscule plastic horse that belongs to her molecule-size horse set. "Someone help me! Help me!"

When Sam gets off the phone, he comes into the living room, where Jayne and I are on our hands and knees, noses to the rug like dogs looking for savory debris. "What's your problem?" he says to me. He picks up a book from the coffee table and throws it across the room. It hits the radiator cover and knocks over a plant that was perched on top. Now there's dirt and broken stalks strewn across the beige wall-to-wall. It's a carpet we never wanted but it came with the house. "I have to answer to alligators all week!" he yells. "It's Sunday. I just wanted to make a few phone calls!"

"I don't get to see you all week," I try to say calmly, "and now you're on the phone talking about Vivian again. Hello? I'm sick of hearing about Vivian."

"He can't date her, Mom," Jayne says, switching her attention to me despite her own problems. "She doesn't date men." Then she gets struck with despair: "Where's my pony?" And she's crying again. And then, in a moment, screaming.

"Dad and I are talking for a minute." I try to remain the only person not yelling. "Jayne, you'll need to leave the room if you can't control yourself."

She clomps out of the room as though she's wearing weighted clogs, then hurls herself onto the carpeted center staircase where she starts madly kicking the risers. "Stop talking and help me!" she screams.

"Can we agree to just drop the subject of Vivian for a while?" I say.

"Who do *you* want to talk about?" he says, and this strikes me as, and I never use this word, *snotty*. Snotty. In general, I can handle many things. But snotty is beyond me.

"Austin," I say. "Let's talk about Austin. I think I'll take him up on his offer."

Jayne is screaming her head off, and I use her voice as a thick curtain behind which I can whisper, "He said he'd take me to the Athenian Diner. He said he'd buy me a meatloaf dinner. With mashed potatoes." I try to sound snotty.

"The gym guy?" Sam sits in a rocker and looks me straight on. "Who is he, anyway?"

"A power lifter."

"How much can he lift?"

"He can lift me into his car and take me to the Athenian Diner." I have my head down because I'm sitting on the carpet, looking for a plastic horse the size of a divided cell.

"You gonna do it?"

"Maybe. When was the last time we had meatloaf."

"I'll make you meatloaf."

"Promise? Next week? Tuesday?"

"I have to give you a date? Christ, Sunny."

I go into the kitchen and take down the kitchen calendar. I sit down on the couch and say, "So, what looks good for you?"

He takes off his sneaker and manages to throw it against the front door, near where Jayne is having her fit. "Quiet!" he yells. "We're trying to help you."

"I have enough people giving me deadlines," he says.

I get up and walk out of the room. I walk upstairs, start the tub even though it's Sunday afternoon, not a time to take a bath. But I don't want to sit in the tub. I just want to lean against it and feel the water pound the sides, feel the force of water move deep into my back.

That night, we sleep together in a parallel, tense union. I fall asleep, but then I wake up and think about Almond Joys. I think *Almond Joy* sounds like a Chinese cookie and not a chocolate coconut candy with a hidden almond inside. I ask myself a question: *If you had never before seen an Almond Joy, and saw the candy for the first time, what would you guess was that round mound?*

"I'm sorry I gave up the trombone," Sam says.

"You're awake?"

"Yes. Are you?" He knows I am. He knows he can always talk to me at night, no matter how late, how early. I am always in a state of wakefulness, unable or unwilling to go under all the way.

"Why are you thinking about the trombone?" I'm mad at him. I'm still waiting for him to give me a date.

"I don't know. I'm sorry I gave it up."

"You can always pick it up."

"No time."

"You're still a trombone player."

"How can I be a player if I don't play?"

"You know, it's like education, a bachelor's, a master's. Or sex. Once you have it, no one can take it away. You're still a trombone player; it's part of you. It's yours."

"You want to have sex?" he asks.

"We've had sex in the past week and no one can take that away from us."

"We can have it again."

"I'm happy with what I have. And I'm tired."

"I think I'll start playing again. A little bit every day."

"Good," I say. "Shh, I'm asleep." But I'm not. I'm wide awake and thinking: If I saw an Almond Joy for the first time, saw the almond bump rising from the chocolate mound, I'd say the bump was a breast. A milk-bearing breast. Rising from the earth.

On Monday, Rae on my back, I walk to the gym and notice autumn. My sister in South Carolina says she misses Connecticut in the fall. "I miss," she wrote recently, "the colors of the leaves against the blue sky." I knew about the leaves, the oranges and the reds; but truly I had forgotten about the blue. I rarely look that far up.

We pass my neighbor, Mrs. Nocera, talking to a friend on the sidewalk. She is wearing a green nylon windbreaker with snaps down the front, just the kind my mother in Ohio is probably wearing this time of year. "Her nose is running," Mrs. Nocera says, looking up at Rae. "Wait a minute." She rummages in the pocket of the windbreaker and pulls out a Kleenex. "It's clean," she says, and reaches up to the back carrier to wipe Rae's nose. Below her jacket hangs an apron imprinted with a huge half of cantaloupe. I haven't seen an apron in ages and I myself have never worn one. Aprons are for those, the older women, who accept their lives and anticipate a stain.

As we approach the gym, Sandy Wargo passes us again in her car. I put up my arm, but I don't raise it high. It's not really a wave; it's more like I'm raising my hand in class but I'm not sure I have the right answer. She is driving with two hands on the wheel and she looks mad. A cigarette is in the dead center of her mouth, sticking straight out. "She'd be better off eating candy," I say to Rae.

In the gym, I pass Rae to Stephanie, who closes her eyes and rubs her nose against Rae's. "Hi, stinker," she says to her.

"Those were beautiful roses the other day," I say. "From your friend at Howard's Discounts?"

"Yeah, except he knows I have a boyfriend. I'm hoping he gave me roses because I gave him a present for his birthday."

"What did you get him?"

"A stripper."

"A stripper?"

"He turned eighteen and we all chipped in."

"Where'd she strip?"

"At Howard's. At the courtesy desk."

"Was she any good?" I ask, trying to sound like a young Howard's employee.

"She was gross. Her underwear looked old and her stomach stuck out. Like from drugs. We could of complained to the company, but she did her job. She was on time and stayed the whole forty-five minutes. She did what we paid her to do."

"You're a good citizen, Stephanie," I say.

I see Austin come in the door wearing red sweatpants and a gray sweatshirt. He waves and we come together at the row of treadmills. We mount our horses and set our course before we begin talking. "So, how's my favorite pioneer woman?" he asks. "Setting a good example for baby in there. Mommy getting strong."

"I'm not always a shining example, believe me," I say.

"I believe nothing."

"Thanks, Austin." I know his name but he doesn't know mine. This is how it is at the gym.

"No, really, girl. You are just fine." He gets off the treadmill. "I do just enough to warm the body. I'm too old for cardio. I just want to lift the world, not make my heart young."

"You're more of a muscle man."

"Work hard," he says. "You have a wagon to drive."

On the way home, Rae sits sleepily in her carrier. Her head is on my shoulder and she's sucking her thumb. I feel her warm weight against my back, her tiny feet at my waist. Because it's cold, I've put tiny sneakers on her, a tiny pink sneak. The laces are threaded with silver and pink. A fairy tale of a shoe and we are both in the story together. *Thumbelina and the Pioneer Rag Woman.*

. . .

It's 7 p.m., and Sam's not home again. I finish the dishes, bathe the girls. Leaning over the tub, I lather, rub, rinse, lean, bend, twist. I cajole, I implore, I admonish. Just turn this way, turn this way, turn this way, turn, turn. Rae is easy to wash. But Jayne is willful. In the fairy tale, Jayne is the girl who rebels, runs away, then regrets the whole thing. I just want her to turn THIS way so I can rinse her hair. When I worked, I didn't have to repeat myself five times. I may have had to ask the next day, or over a period of time, but I didn't have to crouch low in one spot, arms outstretched toward a stubborn object and repeat myself over and over and over.

I really want a Snickers. If I had a solid bar of chocolate and nuts and caramel, maybe I could get them into their pajamas. The roles reverse now. Jayne gets dressed by herself, but Rae runs away and I don't have the energy to ask again or pick her up. I let her stay naked and Jayne and I go downstairs to the living room. Rae comes down the stairs behind us, crawling backward, feet first, looking like a white monkey shimmying down a bamboo tree. Her lily white butt is a fairy tale unto itself, *The Princess and the Precious Butt*, and I realize this even as I am mad and sugar starved.

Jayne plays with some Legos, and Rae crawls on the couch with me. "When's Daddy coming home?" Jayne asks.

"I wish I knew. He doesn't call and he doesn't write."

"Write what?"

"Just an expression."

It's cold outside and it's cold inside. Because the house is old and uninsulated, the cold is free to come and go as it pleases. The chill makes me feel rigid and beat and frosty. I'm lying on the couch, and Rae, totally naked, is sitting on my stomach as though I'm a floor cushion. On the carpet beneath us is what she was wearing before her bath: pink tutu, pink stockings, and pink slippers each with a tuft of fluff and a fabric, pink rosette in the center.

Then she lies down on top of me, her head, neck, naked tummy all close to my face. "Mommy's," she says. She has a single pearl in her hand and I hope it's not mine, hope it's not broken off from my good strand that I left on the hutch in the dining room. She takes the pearl and puts it under my neck, touches it to my forehead. She looks at me with absolute adoration and kisses my cheek. She loses the pearl in the folds of my sweatshirt, then finds it and presses it gently to my chin. We are both in a languorous swoon with each other—the pearl the incidental object of our love and affection.

Sam walks in at seven thirty. "I had a bad day," he says, before I can say anything. Now that he's wrapped himself in the protective sheath of a bad day, there isn't much I can say.

"Can you talk?" he asks.

"Is there anything to say? You had a bad day. I'm tired. I think we've cancelled each other out."

"I'm disappointed. I thought you'd put me in a better mood."

"Sorry to disappoint."

"Is there dinner?"

"On the table. So, I'm a disappointment?"

"Not really. But I was counting on you to boost me a little."

"I was counting on you." I pick up Rae and we start upstairs so I can finally dress her in pajamas. I hear him put his dinner in the microwave, then dial the phone while the oven is humming.

"Who you calling?" I ask from the stairs.

"Hi, Ned," he says. "What's cooking?" He listens for a while, then says, "Not much." Then says, "Guess who I ran into the other day?"

"Give it up!" I shout to him, which sounds to me like *Stick 'em up*, which is more in the spirit of how I feel.

Rae and I continue upstairs. I take her to my room, lie down on my bed, and put her, still naked, on top of me. I throw the covers over the two of us. She holds onto me, her body feeling like a heavy, heated blanket conforming to all my contours and bones and ribs. She is my second skin. Then she starts searching for Ninnie, rubbing her hand on my breast. "No!" I say loudly. "I've had it! Ninnie is sleeping. Give Ninnie a break!" She whimpers, but then puts her head back down on my chest, puts her thumb in her mouth, and closes her eyes.

The next day at the gym, Stephanie has the quiet look of a Sister of Mercy. There are no children in the babysitting room and she is sitting alone in a white, wicker chair, probably a cast-off from Howard's. "Tom quit," she says, when she sees me.

"Why?"

Her face looks drawn and she isn't wearing her usual lipstick or eye liner. "Last night he was supposed to work the courtesy desk but he didn't show, so I called him. He said he doesn't have another job but he had to quit."

"Why?"

"Turns out the stripper was a turn-on for him. Even though she was gross. He took it the wrong way and asked me out. I have a boyfriend. He knows that. But I feel really bad."

"It's amazing how guys misread gestures. Ask a guy to read any-thing—a recipe, the weather forecast—and he thinks it means, *she wants me.*"

"But he doesn't have another job."

"He's eighteen! He has a strong back! Men and women turn each other on all the time. It's nobody's fault."

"Thanks, Sunny," she says, reaching out to take Rae from me. "You're making me feel better." Rae grabs Stephanie's hair and Stephanie says, "Ouch," but doesn't remove Rae's hand. She just takes it. Smiles at Rae. Without her makeup, she looks younger, just a girl herself.

"Would you ever come to our house to babysit?" I ask her. "This Saturday for example?"

Waiting for her to say *Yes* is almost scary. Sam and I share our chil-dren, our bodies, the food on our plates. But we rarely share time to-gether, never see a movie by ourselves or a wedge of sky.

"Yes," Stephanie says. "My boyfriend is riding tractors and I was supposed to take my mother's dog, but I'm not now." I take that as a done deal, and out of the blue my heart starts to pound.

That night Sam comes home early, we get the kids to bed, and at eight thirty we are looking at each other. I never sit and look at him without doing something else at the same time: eating, washing, cooking, folding. His face is always part of a backdrop, the horizon; he is the villa high on the hill—the impending storm, the moon. He is rarely the rowboat or fisherman in the foreground.

"I got a sitter for tomorrow," I say. We are both on the living room couch; I'm sitting in the middle and Sam is lying with his head at one end, his legs draped over my lap like a corduroy afghan.

"I'd love to go away," he says. "Cancun. Florence. Vivian and her partner went to Cancun a few months ago."

I rub his legs gently up and down, up and down, and say to myself a few simple words, *Sam's legs. Sam's legs.* I am putting myself in a Sam trance. Slowly I come back to our conversation. "I guess Vivian and her partner can go anywhere, whenever they have time off."

"Yeah, they've been to Portugal. They did a bike thing through Wales."

"God," I say, not even minding we are talking about her—her whom I loathe, of whom I am insanely jealous. But I am not minding it right now. I am lulled by rubbing his legs and the image of being set free in another country. No one to feed or clothe or bathe but myself. Free hands and a free back. No Ninnie but, instead, my own breasts. Breasts for sex. Then I think of two women together and there it is.

"Did you sleep with her?"

"Who?"

"Vivian."

He puts a hand through his receding curls, then takes one curl at a time and feels it carefully, as though he's fingering fine lingerie. "Okay," he says. "I did. Once. A few times."

"So, you slept with her."

"It was my junior year. I should have gone abroad instead."

I consider getting mad. I want to get mad. I want to throw things just as he's thrown things. I want to break something.

"After Beth and I split, Vivian was just always around. She'd tease me. Take her shirt off or take off her pants. But she didn't want me to do anything. A huge tease. Finally, after a lot of goofing around we did it, but it wasn't good. I thought it was something about me. Crazy, but I kept wanting to try with her. I had this thing where I wanted it to work. I wasn't even sure I liked her. Then she went onto some other guy and that just made me crazier. Then I made all my friends crazy by talking about her."

"You were young. Twenty?"

"I guess. I've thought about her. I wondered why I wanted someone who was so untouchable."

"Did you talk about any of this when you were with her. The other day?"

"No. But she talked about *Cindy*. She wanted me to know."

We sit in the living room, joined together at my lap. I've softened a little, and while I still think of throwing something, I don't want that thing to break.

Here in this house, surrounded by dust, plastic animals, pretend doctor tools, Sam looks joyful. There is a word balloon floating above him which says, *It wasn't me. It was her. She was gay all along.* He has been resurrected.

Funny, but now I'm jealous of Sam. No matter what else is amiss in his life, he has this for now. This piece of his life, rewritten, which recasts his history in a merciful light.

The next day it's raining lightly and I drive to the gym. Rae is in her car seat in the back. As I enter the Waldbaum's Plaza, I see Sandy Wargo driving into the lot, a cigarette sticking straight out of her mouth. I honk and roll down my window. She looks mad but stops anyway and rolls down hers. She leaves the cigarette in her mouth and just sits still, waiting for me.

"You were right about candy," I tell her. "I think a candy fundraiser is a good idea. Lately, all I want is candy. I'd like some candy right now." I laugh a little so she won't be inclined to reach down into her breasts and pull out a pistol.

She doesn't answer me but instead reaches into the back seat. For a few seconds, I'm scared. I think maybe she *does* have a pistol. Or that she'll pull out a shopping list, study it in front of me, then drive away as though I'd never said a word. As though I'm so small, so thin voiced, I'm not here.

Instead, she turns around holding in her hand a Mounds bar.

"You like coconut?"

"Love it."

"Here." Her voice is muffled. Her cigarette is moving up and down and seems to be talking for her.

She tries to hand over the Mounds through her car window but our cars are not quite close enough, so she has to get out. She looks aggravated as she slowly twists and lifts her body out of the driver's seat. "Here," she says again. She has taken the cigarette out of her mouth and extends the candy, which I take.

"You like the kind with the nut?" she asks. "The almond kind?"

"Yes."

She opens the back door of her car and reaches across the seat. When she turns around, she has an Almond Joy in her hand. "Don't say I never gave you nothin.'"

"I won't," I say, my heart singing.

She gets back in her car and drives farther into the plaza, her black Camaro blasting exhaust at me.

I look at my big Almond Joy, the blue and brown lettering, the length of it. I look at the wrapper. "*Candy is patient. Candy is kind,*" I say to Rae, remembering a passage about love from the Bible, from Corinthians. It's something priests say at weddings. Actually a priest said it at ours.

"*Candy is not self-seeking. Candy is not prone to anger.*" I picture a priest speaking of love, offering these words to the bride and groom, their faces in white light and turned toward him. They must be thinking, "If only we can remember this, we can win." *There is no limit to its hope, its power to endure.* The newlyweds are listening so hard, they are squinting.

Stephanie shows up before five that evening. She hoists Rae onto her hip, as though she's her own, as though we are all members of a commune and picking up Rae is part and parcel of being a Bruderhof or Hutterite. Jayne is sitting cross-legged under the Queen Anne table with her head ducked low. She is hiding, smiling, waiting to be found. We are all in love and shy around Stephanie, who is neither a relative nor close friend but still one of us.

Sam and I drive to Essex, so we can sit by the water and pretend we are in Florence. It is cold. Wearing heavy, hooded sweatshirts, we sit on Steamboat Dock, on a bench, and look out. Before us, the river is bigger, more expansive than we are. The sky is bigger, and the geese, flying above us in twilight, are higher. There is something about looking out and up. What a relief to look out. What we see is not us. We hold hands. I feel his pulse. We are here for now.

Communion

WHEN SAM CAME HOME that evening, he saw, on the steps of his front porch, a stranger laughing into a cell phone. He parked the car in the driveway and looked at the person laughing. She registered with him as a strange woman, but at the same time he was replaying something he had just said to his boss, something about looking beyond the fat in a fat person he'd just interviewed. His boss claimed not to understand what Sam meant. "How do you look beyond fat?" the boss said. "You look behind one, you see another. Two in one. Like Doublemint gum."

"But one stick," Sam said. "Doublemint is one stick of gum. I interviewed one person of gum."

"I disagree," the boss said. "Two people. Okay two, *equal* people, but one is a ticking liability."

"Just one stick, though," Sam said, aware he didn't have the words to further his argument. Then the boss said he had to go, which meant Sam, too, had to go. Now he was sitting in his car, in his driveway, thinking about a fat woman who couldn't get even one shift at the fish counter. And thinking the boss was wrong. The boss had it wrong, and the boss won.

Sam got out of his car and walked to the front of his house. The stranger on his porch was a young woman who sat like a man, her legs spread and confident in loose jeans. He knew he didn't know her and he knew Sunny didn't know her. The woman had a top, side tooth that rested on her bottom lip and short blond hair that looked unwashed. He gave some thought how he would walk past her—confident and casual, he decided. This was his house. Yet as he walked by, he felt shy. She had big thighs.

Sunny, his wife, was standing by the door looking out. Sam said, "Excuse me," to the woman, who didn't seem to notice him, even when he had to step over her arm outstretched on the top step.

"No, not just candy corn and wax lips," she said into the phone. "I feed them other things. Chicken, noodles. Come get me, Gooch. I'm hungry."

"Who's she?" Sam whispered to Sunny as he walked in the front door.

"My God, Sam, I know. She's so sad." Sunny was whispering because they were in the front foyer, close to the front door where the woman was. "She's a mother I run into at Peasley School."

Sunny's whispers were full of faint hisses and *s* sounds—the sound of someone chewing and popping gum. Because he couldn't understand what Sunny was saying, he tried, instead, to read her face—her light brows rising, the slight bulb at the tip of her nose turning red.

"She walked by the house as I was shaking out rugs." Sam didn't get it. He had the idea of putting his whole head into her mouth to understand her. "What?" he said.

"She said her car is broken and her hip is smashed. She unloads steel doors at Home Express and a steel door fell on her."

"Why's she on our steps?"

"She was on pain meds because the steel door crushed her hip. The meds made her high and she crashed her car. Now she's walking home from the body shop."

"Why's she on our steps?"

"She's trying to make it home. She's tired and her hip hurts. I told her to sit and I'd bring her a soda." Sunny had her hand on Sam's shoulder and had her mouth to his ear so she could whisper. Her breath was like a yellow buttercup. He thought of girls putting buttercups under his chin and asking, "You like butter?" He loved butter.

"What are we going to do with her?" he asked.

"I'll give her a soda and offer her a ride."

"So, get the soda."

"I don't know if we have any soda."

"Then what are you going to give her?" All the whispering made him realize he was dry, thirsty, and likely had bad breath. "Do I have bad breath?" he asked her.

"No," she said in a breathy whisper. He loved that he could ask her if he had bad breath and later ask her for butter. He could say, *Do I smell? Am I dirty?* And she'd smile and always say, *No.* Or, *No* with a swooning roll of the eyes, as though she was ready to keel over from the smell of dirt. But he couldn't whisper more questions now because the whispering was hard on his throat and he was thirsty. He wanted to talk normally. He wanted dinner. He wanted the kids to go to bed and he wanted to tell Sunny about the woman applicant and the boss.

"What are you going to get her?" he asked, this time above a whisper. Almost full voice.

"Shhh," she said. "Diet lemonade. With a lot of ice."

"Then get it." He was getting angry now. He walked from the foyer into the dining room, where he put his briefcase on the table, his jacket on the back of a chair. Sunny went into the kitchen and opened one cabinet after another. Then she opened the refrigerator, but he couldn't see her because she was on her knees, probably sticking her whole head in and looking at the slotted shelves from below.

He walked partway into the living room to say hi to the girls but they didn't say hi back. They were watching TV, Rae sitting cross-legged on the linty rug, Jayney standing before the set. Rae was wearing a white diaper and a white turtleneck with red stains down the front. She looked to Sam like a bare-legged butcher. Her thumb was in her mouth and, as always, the thumb struck him as a breast. Rae had loved Sunny's breast and now she loved her own thumb. Breast and thumb were the same to her and he understood that, since he himself was a breast and thumb man. He didn't suck his thumb anymore, but with a file and clippers he groomed it a lot.

Next to Rae, six-year-old Jayney was moving to *The Simpsons*. She was bending at the waist, bobbing wildly, and she was pumping her arms and hands over to her right side. With her head and torso bobbing, she might have been mimicking an Orthodox Jew; but with her arms working off to one side, she could equally be rowing a canoe. The big giveaway was her lips, puckered as though waiting for a kiss. And, also, Lisa Simpson playing the sax.

He walked to the far end of the living room, toward the TV. "Hi?" he said. Rae didn't take her thumb out. She didn't even look up. Jayney shook her head from side to side, as someone blowing into a sax might signal a hi.

He finished his circle around the downstairs, going into the tiny pantry area and back into the kitchen. His shirt, he noticed, had ink on it. He had an anxious feeling, almost panic, that he was a white shirt with ink. The shirt was walking and the shirt's heart was beating fast. He had the idea of giving the girls each a pen and telling them to write on him. Maybe they would have a rare, insightful thought that he was inside.

He didn't say excuse me to Sunny as he leaned over her to pull out a beer from the refrigerator. He knew he was rude, but a stranger, camped out and comfortable on his porch, was the object of Sunny's attention.

To streamline his stress and make things easier on himself, he decided to be mad at Sunny. "You gonna find that lemonade or what?" he asked.

The phone rang. It was Sister Anne from across the street. "There's a woman sitting on your front porch," said Sister Anne.

"Yes?" said Sam.

"I know her. Do you know her?"

"Sunny says her kids go to Peasley School and Sunny knows who she is."

"How much does Sunny know about her?"

"All I know is we're looking to give her a cold drink because her car broke down and a steel door fell on her."

"I know her son, Franklin, from communion," Sister Anne said. "If you need any help let me know."

From the other side of the refrigerator, still hidden from view, he heard Sunny saying, "For the love of dirt!"

"Do you have a Coke?" Sam asked. "Sunny wants to give her soda or lemonade."

"We always have some soda around."

"Could we borrow some?"

"I'll bring it over."

Sunny came into view. From her squatting position, she put her arms behind her and leaned backward, so she was nearly on her back in front of the refrigerator. Sam gave her a hand and helped her up. "Ouch!" she yelled, and he realized he had pulled a little too hard.

"Who's she talking to on the cell phone?" Sam asked.

"Someone who's amusing the heck out of her. She seems to be acting coy and come-hither."

"On our porch?" Sam asked.

Sunny shrugged and put up her hands as if to say, It's out of my hands.

"Does she live near here?" Sam asked, but was afraid to know. "Is she a neighbor?"

"She's desperate and pathetic. Of course she's our neighbor."

Now he was angry at Sunny for saying that someone who lived near him was desperate and pathetic. For so much as saying he made a bad choice buying this house, for suggesting that anyone who lived within a two- to three-mile radius was a recognized deadbeat. His father didn't flat-out tell him not to buy it. He had said, instead, "Use your head. Think. You don't want to be the best house on the block." But Sam and Sunny had liked the built-ins, the brick fireplace, the sunroom. And it had been recently painted. All this was good, especially when you already had two little girls and your apartment lease was up.

"Where's she live?" Sam asked.

"The other side of Spring Street. She was married to this nice, mixed guy. They're not together anymore but she sometimes sleeps at his house, on the sofa, so she can get the kids off to school in the morning. She herself is staying with some woman, who I think takes care of her."

Sam felt she had this information and was bullying him with it. He shook his head and felt the very top of his skull, the crown, aching and throbbing. In books, you always read about a throbbing penis. But it was his head that throbbed. Eventually, he thought, the pain would work its way down and his penis would have the headache. One day he'd be at work and blurt out, "Man, my penis has a throbbing headache."

"Tell me again, exactly, why she's here?" he asked.

"Her car, her hip. She's poor, she's close to homeless."

"You know her whole story," he said. He said this only because he thought it was the end of the story. He wanted the story to end. But Sunny had more.

"One time she asked if I could give a ride to her little boy who had child care at the Y. Her car was in the shop and she had no way to get him there. The boy sat in back in Rae's car seat and she sat in front."

"Where was Rae?"

"Child care."

Sam wouldn't say, *We pay money for Rae to go to child care so you can take this other kid to child care?* Instead he said, "So, you are now the designated driver?" He tried for a tone of humor, with an undertone of nastiness.

The doorbell rang and it was Sister Anne. "I have Sunkist orange," she called out. "Do you have a glass and some ice?"

"Come in," Sunny called.

Sister Anne came in, a tall, six-footer of a nun, and Sunny gave her a hug. "I just passed our friend on the porch. How you doing?"

"My knees stink, but otherwise I'm okay. You have a glass?"

Sunny started getting everything together, and Sister Anne said, "Do you know who this girl is?"

"Who?" Sunny and Sam said.

"Don't say you heard it from me. Just don't say, period. Her name is Francesca. She lit a match and burned one of her kids, little Franklin. What she told me was she was mad at him because he got her into trouble with the Y. They scolded her because Franklin wasn't wearing socks and the Y has a sock rule. The kids have to wear socks because they take off their shoes in the daycare room and they don't want them barefoot. Francesca claims he had socks when she brought him, but he took them off. She was afraid they'd report her to the state for the socks. She thought that might be considered abuse. So what does she do? She burns him. She gets mad at him for the socks and lights a match or a lighter and burns his leg. The state took him away and put him in a foster home. But I think he's back living with his father."

"Oh, great," Sam said.

"How badly was he burned?" Sunny was now holding a glass filled with ice and orange soda.

"A blister burn. Second degree. He took off his Band-Aid and showed everyone his big blister during circle time."

"Who's Gooch?" Sam asked.

"Beats me." Sunny took the glass of orange soda to the front door and with her free hand knocked before she came out. Sam and Sister Anne watched her. Francesca looked up at the soda being handed to her, but didn't stop talking and didn't seem to say thank you. Sam saw Sunny talk to her and Francesca put her hand over the phone and answered Sunny back.

Sunny returned to the kitchen. "She'll take a sandwich. And some tomato soup."

"You feed her and she might not ever leave," the sister said.

"What can I do?" said Sunny. The three of them were standing in front of the refrigerator. It made Sam sad that whenever the sister came over, they always leaned or stood, never sat. For one thing, the kitchen was too small for a table and chairs. For another, time in this home was never leisurely. It was always food, dishes, diapers, clothes, hop, hop, hop till you drop. Sometimes, and especially now that it was October, they could take a bike ride to the funeral home.

"Let's chip in and give her money for a meal," said the sister.

"I don't know her," said Sunny. "She might use the money for drugs. Oh, and she doesn't have a car."

"Damn, you're right," said Sister Anne. She hugged her arms to her chest. "Okay, tell her you'll feed her and call her a cab. Don't drive her anywhere. And I'll pay for the cab."

"I'll pay for the cab," said Sam. "But you know what?" He paused. "Could you hurry with that sandwich, Sunny? I want her gone and you know, frankly, I'm hungry too."

"Of course you are," said Sister Anne. "The man has to eat. Hey, look. You could come over to our house for dinner. Sister Ancillita is making a roast."

Sam pictured a nice china plate, a glass of wine, the evening news on the large screen. The sisters' home was a spiritual place. Always warm, always a piece of cake for dessert, the cross on the wall, Jim Lehrer on TV.

"Wouldn't that be nice!" said Sunny. She looked to one side. "Warm roast. Meat."

"Remind me to tell you about the meat man," Sam said, hoping to get Sunny's attention.

"The meat man from work?" Sister Anne said. "You still having trouble with that guy? Send him over here."

He loved Sister Anne. He wanted to sit down at her table and tell her about the meat man, the fish man, his boss, the poor overweight applicant. "I love roast," Sam said. "But we have a guest on our porch and we can't leave." He could smell the roast now on Sister Anne's large block of a white blouse.

"I'll tell you what," Sister Anne said. "I'll bring you two over a plate. Have the kids eaten?"

"Yes," said Sunny.

"Frankly," Sam said, keeping his voice low and looking around, "I want this woman gone as soon as possible. I don't want everyone driving by seeing her sitting on our step talking to this Gooch. It looks like our house is turning into another rooming house."

"That's all we need," said Sister Anne. Across the street from Sam and Sunny and next door to the Sisters of Mercy was a rooming house. Forsaken men lived there. They sat on the wide porch steps, in full view, broadcasting their various stages of pickling or psychosis. When Sam looked out his living room window, he didn't see lawns or trees. He saw these men, sitting on the porch. It killed him.

Ten years ago, when Sunny and Sam bought their house, the rooming house was an elegant, commanding, single home, a 1920s colonial with a full front porch and ornate columns. But the couple who lived there divorced, and the house was bought by a wealthy rooming house magnate. He converted the single family into single rooms, each room occupied by a disabled man on state assistance. The boarders were thirty-, forty-, fifty-year-old men, acting as though they were on their own for the first time and seeing what they could get away with: pissing outside and seeing if mom would come out and yell; drinking 7 UP out of a paper bag and baiting a cop to stop. "Only 7 UP, officer. Sorry for your inconvenience." Sam had been mowing his lawn once when he saw this happen. After the cop left, the guy called out to Sam, "Hey, I'll do this for one month then switch to gin. Got to train these guys." Sam didn't look at him, but gave him a wave.

There was the other guy who picked up the discarded stuff Sam had put on the side of the road—battered chairs from college, broken bookcases, supermarket drinking glasses. Sam was giving the stuff away free. But it galled him that the guy then sold the giveaways at his own weekly rummage sale. Sam named him *Rummage.*

Then there was the guy, all hair and bones, who spent hours sitting motionless at the edge of the rooming house sidewalk. He had a long spindly beard that came down to his chest, and the sisters called him *Moses.* And he often hit up the sisters for money. Which they gave him.

"Look, you guys sit tight," said Sister Anne. "Sunny, make Francesca a sandwich and I'll be back with your dinner."

Sunny kissed her cheek and Sister Anne said, "We'll take care of Miss Tough Nut. Don't worry. You'll get your dinner and she'll be gone by eight." Sunny and Sam escorted Sister Anne to the front door and opened it for her. Sister Anne looked down at her feet, careful where she placed them. She looked worried she might step on Francesca, who was now semi-reclined on the step and saying, "You gonna take me out for dinner, Gooch?"

Sister Anne gave Francesca a little wave as she tiptoed around her, and Francesca took the phone away from her ear and said, "Sister, I didn't know you lived across the street. In a normal house."

"What can I say? We are normal sisters."

"Right. My baby, Franklin, really loves you, sister."

"He's a cute little boy. Eager to please."

"He's very important to me."

"I'm sure of it, hon." She waved to Francesca as she walked down the front walk to the street. Sister Anne waited at the edge of the walk until two trucks and a motorcycle passed. Sunny and Sam watched her from the front door as she crossed the street and made it safely to her own home.

"Goochie, guess what?" Francesca said into the phone. "The nun from Communion was just here." She put one leg close to her chest and draped an arm around it. "Hey, she lives across the street here. I didn't know that. It's a regular house. Two story. I thought they lived in a nunnery. Hey, Gooch. Get thee to a nunnery, right?"

Sunny left to make the sandwich and Sam stood near the door, listening to her, watching her drink her soda. "I graduated high school," Francesca said into the phone. "I left home and I finished on my own. With honors. You didn't know this about me, did you?"

Jayney came to the door, still holding her imaginary sax and bobbing like a pecking chicken, her lips still ready for a kiss. Sam kissed her and said, "You didn't say hi."

"Who's that?" Jayney said, lifting up the sax and pointing it out the front door.

"Someone Mom knows," Sam said.

"Who is she?" Jayney asked.

"I told you, I don't know. Someone Mom knows."

"Mom, who is she?" Jayney called out.

Sunny walked into the foyer and said, "Shhh. She's a mother and a sad person. Come away from the door."

"What's she doing here?" Jayney said.

"That's my question," said Sam.

"Shhh," Sunny said, from her dark spot in the foyer. "Her car is broken. She's been walking all over town. Her hip is hurt and she's hungry."

"I don't know what you guys are talking about," said Jayney. "I want to ride my bike."

"No one is leaving the house," Sam said, "until that woman is gone."

Jayney started to cry. "Why can't I go outside with my bike? Who is she?"

"Sunny, I want her gone," Sam said.

"I'll hurry with the sandwich."

They all left the door and went into the kitchen. Sunny brought out a skillet, started heating it with butter. The butter made Sam hungry, but not for sex. Just for butter. A grilled cheese sandwich. Sunny nuked some soup and put it on a tray, along with another glass of orange soda.

"Lucky her," Sam said, standing in the kitchen door. "Maybe I should sit on the porch and act all down-and-out. Maybe I'll talk to Gooch."

"Excuse me," said Sunny, looking disgusted, pushing him away from the refrigerator so she could open it. Sam didn't know if she looked disgusted because of Francesca or because of him.

He watched her make the sandwich, add it to the tray, and walk through the dining room to the foyer. Jayney and Rae were together now standing by the front door. Rae's hair looked sweaty. The two girls stared at the tray, wanting to know who the woman was and when she was leaving. "Everyone give me some space," Sunny said, as she walked to the front door.

"That sandwich looks good," said Jayney. "And we never get tomato soup. You never make *me* tomato soup."

"Everybody step back, please," said Sunny. "Go back in the living room. Sam, take them into the living room. Or better yet, go upstairs. Start their baths."

"We never get anything on that tray, either," said Jayney. She was standing right at the front door, watching her mother stop in the dining room for a napkin. "Where'd you get that tray, Mommy? I didn't know you had that tray."

"Goochie, they're bringing me a tray with food," Francesca said. "They're better than you. I don't even know them and they're bringing me food."

"I want to go outside," Jayney said. "It's too early for my bath."

Rae stood by her sister's side, sucking her thumb. Her diaper looked low and full, and with one hand she fingered a bit of fine hair behind her ear.

"Sam," Sunny said again. She sounded militant. "Get them upstairs, please. And baths!"

He was starving and didn't want to start baths. Baths weren't supposed to come for another hour. There was supposed to be dinner and a bike ride to the funeral home. That was the routine and that's what he wanted. Then he saw Sister Anne leaving her house, carrying a big tray with an array of foil-covered packets. He didn't want to leave his food. It would be here any minute. He wanted to count the seconds it took her to cross the road.

Sunny knocked on the front door slightly with her foot, so Francesca would look up and open the door for her. As Francesca stood up, Sam could see how broad she was. She had big shoulders, big boots. She wore a white button-down shirt tucked into jeans and her waist was small, her hips big. "Sam," Sunny said, softening her voice. "Please take the kids upstairs?"

"My dinner is coming," he said. Sister Anne was crossing the street now, looking both ways for cars, holding the tray tightly.

"You have food coming for me, from both sides," said Francesca. "Look at the big tray the nun is carrying. It's fuckin' Thanksgiving here."

"That's for me," Sam said. He was holding the door partway open and talking to her. "Sunny's tray is for you."

"Which is better?" Francesca said. "Don't I get to choose?"

Sam couldn't tell if she was trying to smile or smirk.

"Well, the one coming across the street is for me and Sunny."

"Sunny, is that your name? You drove me to the Y that time and I never knew your name."

"Her real name is Katherine," Sam said. "We only sometimes call her Sunny. Like when we're hungry and she's busy."

"You messin' with me?" Francesca asked.

"He's joking," said Sunny. "Don't spill the soup," she said to Francesca. "I have here grilled cheese, soup, and soda."

Sister Anne was on the sidewalk now looking at her feet again and trying to navigate her way up the porch stairs. Sam opened the door and walked down the steps with his arms outstretched for the tray.

"Wait a minute," said Francesca. "Hey, excuse me, Miss Nun. Who's your tray for?"

"For Sam and Sunny."

"Her name *is* Sunny. What's this Katherine shit? You were messin' with me. You think I'm stupid. I don't need your fucking food. Forget it." She sat down on the porch steps and resumed talking into her phone. "These people are fucking with me. Come get me, Gooch. Let's see." She stood, turning to face the brass house numbers on the front door. "740 High Street. Come fast. I'm outside on their fucking steps. I'm fucking starving."

"You're not going to eat the food?" Sunny said.

"I ain't eatin' nothin' you got to give me. Thanks, anyway. Unless I eat the nun's food. I'll eat her food."

"No way," said Sam. He had walked past her into the house. He stood behind the door now, holding the tray, and spoke to her through the glass. "Sorry, but I'm hungry, too."

"Look, I'll eat the grilled cheese," said Sunny in a soft voice, bending down low to Francesca, as though whispering to her now. "And you and Sam can split the roast beef."

"I ain't sharin' nothing with him," Francesca said.

"Sorry, hon," said Sister Anne. "These people are nice enough to let you stay here till your ride comes, but they're hungry too. I brought the tray for them."

"Let them have it," Francesca said. She pushed over to one side of the steps and turned her face toward the shrubs.

"I'll stay a while," said Sister Anne.

"Thank you, sister," said Francesca. She pulled out a pack of cigarettes and shook one out. Behind the glass front door, Sam kept still, keeping watch over her. Rae was somewhere behind him. He could hear her sucking her thumb. Sunny and Sister Anne were on the porch and Sam didn't like this. He wished Sunny and Sister Anne were both inside with the kids and him. Francesca. Sounded like an Italian princess. Was there, he thought, a Princess Francesca? This Francesca was a study in slow movements and he felt fixed in his spot, even as he still held the tray. She took then from her breast pocket a lighter.

"Can you not do that here?" Sunny asked. "The cigarettes and lighter upset my children."

Francesca said nothing. Instead she stood up, put the pack of cigarettes and lighter back in her front shirt pocket, then hit her chest to smooth the fabric. She began to sit down again, but then whirled around fast and in one ferocious move punched the door. The glass shattered and made a screaming pop. Sam jumped out of the way but still got sprayed by glass. He'd seen fights. And he'd fought when he was a kid. *Keep your head*, his father always said. Which meant what, Sam thought back then.

The tray had glass in it, too, and he rushed to put it down. But she had already opened the door by the handle and punched the tray out of his hands. Her hands and wrists were bleeding. Foil packets flew, and juice sprayed out. A foil-wrapped ball, looking like a big silver egg, hit Rae's bare foot. She kept the thumb in her mouth but opened her mouth around it and screamed. Saliva ran down her chin.

Inside the front hall, his hands free now, he grabbed Francesca and pinned her arms to her side. She was squirming and twisting but he was taller and in a rage equal to hers. "Open the door," he said in a restrained fervor to Sunny. He was trying to keep his voice as low as possible, so the girls wouldn't get further panicked. As he brought Francesca outside he said, "Sorry, sister," to Sister Anne, who had to back away to make room for the struggling pair. "Call the police, Sunny," he said.

He got Francesca down the steps, gripping her with all his might. He might have had glass on his hands, too, but he didn't look, didn't care. He wanted to bloody her mouth and nose, to pummel her but instead put all his strength into a massive squeeze. He brought her to the sidewalk, not knowing what to do with her then.

He looked across the street, where, on the front steps of the rooming house, the rummage sale dealer was watering potted plants. "Need some help, man?" Rummage shouted.

"I'm okay," yelled Sam.

"I'm bleeding," Francesca said.

"I'll come over," Rummage called out.

"Christ, that's all I need," Sam said under his breath.

"Me, too," said Francesca, who was rocking her shoulders with enormous strength and making furious attempts at breaking free. Sam got her to the ground and was not so much restraining her as hugging her. She was squirming, trying to use her shoulders to break free of him, and he could do nothing, it seemed, but hug her.

Rummage crossed over to the sidewalk and looked down at Francesca, who was writhing under Sam, arching her back, trying to throw him off. "Let's divide her," Rummage said. "I'll take the bottom, you take the top." He sat at her feet, put her legs over his, and leaned over using all his weight. Sam moved to the top of her head, linked his arms through hers and pinned her elbows against the sidewalk. He'd been good with his fists, but never wrestled. And here he was, feeling like a cowboy trying to rope a stranger.

"You call the cops, buddy?" Rummage asked.

"Sunny did."

"They come fast. Hey, if you keep it up," he said to Francesca, "I'll sit on you."

"Gooch is comin' to get me," Francesca said, still squirming. "He'll get here before the cops."

"Oh, Gooch," Rummage said. "Gooch? Gooch comin'? Good. We'll take him out, too."

Behind him, Sam heard Jayney and Rae crying. He heard Sunny say, "It's okay. It's okay. The woman's getting help." He heard Sister Anne say, "Don't worry, girls. She's harmless." And Sam, aware now of a drumming in his head, was grateful that his neighbor had come and taken Francesca's lower half, the part with the bad hip. Sam didn't want the bad hip, but he wanted the hip damaged. He closed his eyes and could only feel his arms straining and the hardness of her muscles. Blood from her hands and wrists had stained his shirt, and he thought if he could only take off the shirt, he could either stop her bleeding or smother her. But he couldn't let go of his hold.

"Sunny!" he called. "Get me a blanket."

A blanket. Before the cops arrived, he would roll her in a blanket, like she was on fire, a fire ball, and he would roll her and roll her as long as it took to put her out.

Father Guards the Sheep

THIS HAPPENED IN the early eighties, when I disbelieved anything not in my best interest. Disbelief afforded me the freedom of a fresh square one. Whose truth was truer, anyway: Was I fired from Greystone Park Psychiatric in New Jersey? Or mainstreamed into the world-at-large to pursue new directions?

Who's to say I wasn't executive assistant to the fire chief in Palo Alto?

"I was the executive assistant to the fire chief in Palo Alto," I told the chief of the New Haven Arson Squad. He held my resume in his big hands, but he looked up at me. The interview was in a new office smelling of fresh paint, with a trace underlay of flame retardant in children's pajamas. "But God knows California is a long way from Connecticut. And I wanted to be near my mother, who lives not thirty minutes from here." When the chief turned from me to retrieve a file, I was emboldened by his broad back, his wrinkled, white shirt. "My father," I falsely noted, "was a firefighter."

I was scared he'd call Palo Alto to check on me. Check in with Chief Clay, a name I thought up when thinking of hobbies I'd enjoyed as a kid. I made up a phone number, too, and wondered the odds of the name and number matching up. I was more nervous my supervisor at Greystone Park had put my name into a national file of regretfully dismissed employees. I'd already crafted what I would say to the chief if my Greystone Park dismissal surfaced.

I'm so sorry if I misled anyone. Yes, Palo Alto wasn't really in the picture. I know it was wrong not to mention what happened to me at Greystone Park but, frankly, I wasn't cut out for that line of work. I did once apply for an office job at a fire department, but they thought of me as more of a doer than a strict "do-as-you're-told" person. In retrospect, they were right. If I had to name one fault, it's that I take on more than I'm asked to do.

I considered simplifying the story, but days after the Arson Squad interview, as I burrowed under the coffee-colored afghan on my mother's couch, I got a call from the chief. I had won out over the other top candidates. "You're a bit of spitfire, aren't you," he said.

So there.

And there I was. Behind the front desk of a brand-new, model program in New Haven—Arson Warning and Prevention Strategy. AWAPS. You pronounced it A-WAPS. It rhymed with stay straps—the clasps that keep your bra straps from slipping. I told the chief I preferred not answering the phone, "AWAPS." It sounded like AWOL—like, he went AWOL. And if the caller heard WOL, he might think WAC—like she was in the WACS, and WACS was only a stone's throw from WIC, the food program. And if the caller heard WIC he'd think he reached the social services department.

"You might be getting at something," the chief said, looking first at me, then down at the new brown carpeting. "But our stationary says *AWAPS.* The fire personnel, the police, the housing people, they all call us *AWAPS.*" He had large hips, a large body, and when he stood before me, he scared me a little.

The job scared me a little too. I was a research assistant. More specifically, I was a soothsayer. I was to follow a research protocol that allowed me to predict, each month, which city houses a landlord might want to torch. When it came to arson, in New Haven, it would come down to me. And as my mother would say, "There's no telling." No telling if I would fuck up again. But I would try not to.

"*They* can call us A-WAPS," I said. In my office chair, I sat as tall as my small body allowed. "But when I pick up the phone, I'd like to be able to say, instead, 'Arson Warning and Prevention. May I help you?'"

He wrapped his arms in front of his chest and set them in the lock position.

I pushed through. "They might, to their ear, think I'm saying, EX-LAX."

I didn't think I was joking, but he laughed. Then he unfurled his large arms and lay his hands before me, palms up. Burt Lancaster in *Birdman of Alcatraz*, beckoning a bird to alight. "It's your party," he said.

He had made me the hostess. And I swore to myself I would serve him. I would offer him party food—Velveeta and lobster chunks in hot dog buns; Manhattans in frosted flutes. For I believed, I truly believed, I could be helpful to him. And if I couldn't help, I believed I could charm my way out, disarm the Arson Squad with my youth and candor.

I didn't believe I was pregnant when I announced this to my mother, but I was blindsided by the setting sun. We were having dinner on the screened-in porch, and the sun blasting through the wooden shades was like fixed streaks of lightening. I'd been trying to savor the food she'd made—a silken macaroni and cheese topped with crumbled, buttered potato chips. The sun was interfering with the experience of eating a plateful of heaven with my mother. Then my mother started interfering with the experience of being with my mother.

"This arson thing seems to be working out," she said.

"Seems to," I said, but it hurt my eyes to look at her. "The sun."

"I know. It didn't do this years ago. We'd eat out here, remember? And the sun never bothered us."

It was true. Summers we always ate out here, the two of us. I missed my father, but didn't say so and she didn't say, either. We never wondered out loud why he left, his leaving not altogether strange or unexpected. When he came to say goodnight to me, he'd stand in the door to my room, but wouldn't step in. *Schlaf, Kindlein, Schlaf,* he'd sing. German words he never taught me.

The sun was killing me, and I left the table to get my sunglasses. When I returned, my mother was putting more macaroni on my plate. "I know this is your favorite," she said.

"I love it."

"Is the job secure?"

"Whoever knows."

"The chief seems to like you."

"I like him, too," I said. "I compliment him on his work and he compliments me and we go on like that. You just have to set things in motion and it comes back around."

"Speaking of motion," she said.

Instinctively, I held my breath.

"Now may be a good time for you to casually start checking out apartments closer to the fire department. Besides, it's a thirty-five-minute drive from here to New Haven."

"You think I've been here long enough?"

"You've heard me say this house is really too big for me. When your father was here, and you, it seemed big. But." She'd stopped eating her macaroni, and what remained on her plate looked like a stony mound of construction rubble.

"You want to move?" I asked her.

"No. I want to stay. Armand would move in. That's what we're thinking. He'd run his heating and cooling business from here."

For years, I tried to disbelieve Armand. In college, in our weekly phone calls, my mother often mentioned him. But he was just a mention, not a real-life, breathing, heating-and-cooling person.

"The den could be a kind of ante room, and your room, I was thinking, could be the office. We'd get a good Selectric, phone, files, copy machine. The rest of the house would remain the rest of the house."

"Only with Armand in it," I said.

"If you wanted or needed to stay here, you are always welcome. We have the rec room. It has that nice heater now and the linoleum."

I didn't want to be welcomed. I wanted to be here, a proper and named resident. I wanted my home.

Even with sunglasses, my eyes burned and teared.

"So, what do you think?" my mother asked.

"I'm glad for Armand's plans. But I have a big problem."

"What, hon?"

"I might be pregnant." I paused and reconsidered. "Actually, I am pregnant."

"Oh my God. By the chief?"

"No!"

"By who then?"

"You don't know the guy and it doesn't matter. It's just that I am and I would never, you know."

"You're pregnant?"

"I guess I'll go the whole way and have it."

"I don't believe it. I just can't believe it. I can't believe you're pregnant. My God, Esther. Pregnant. Unbelievable. What are you going to do?"

"Have the baby."

"Where?"

"Here, I was hoping. But now we have a Selectric and files going on."

"I don't get it," she said, looking down at her lap, as though she herself was in trouble. "First you leave Greystone Park. And that was a good job. Right up your alley, right? You tell me you're just using up vacation time, but then you never go back? And now?"

"I could go on assistance and get my own apartment. But I don't know the first thing about babies."

"I'm no expert. I only had you."

I chewed a little. She looked at the slats. "How many months?"

"Just one."

"They generally don't consider you on track until you're two to three months."

"Okay then. We'll wait and see."

I didn't expect to cry just then, in the same way I didn't expect to announce a pregnancy. The cry came from somewhere I couldn't grasp, but there it was overtaking me.

"Alright," she said, as in no, it's not alright. She sat up straight, her mouth tight and composed, as if scared to have a photo taken. "Let's see what happens." She got up from the table to leave and put her hand over mine. "Esther," she said. "Oh, Esther," as in, what is the universe throwing at me this time? "I'll be back," she said walking out of the porch.

I waited for her, but she never came back to me. I found her on our living room sofa, asleep and fully dressed, her eyeglasses on. I slipped off the glasses, her terry slip-ons, then didn't know what else to remove. I went to my own room. My candy-striped curtains would go. The pink and red pom-pom spread would go. Armand would take up where I left off, and me? Alone with a baby.

The people at Greystone Park Psychiatric hired me, straight out of college, to be an outreach worker. My job was to check in on clients who'd been discharged from the big hospital to small outpatient homes— Good Faith House, Earth House, Shepard Home. I would conduct group check-in meetings and spend time with the residents, most of whom were chronic schizophrenics forgotten by their families, psychiatrists, inpatient therapists. "Just take care of their basic needs," my supervisor told me over and over. "Let the meds do the work."

So, I was the caretaker for basic needs. And if you leave it to me, basic goes beyond supportive footwear, white sport socks, and a steady diet of psychotropic zines so cutting edge in the eighties: Thorazine, Stelazine, Compazine. I wanted to give my people things higher up on the pyramid than jog pants with wide waistbands, housedresses with snap plackets.

So, when shopping at Bamberger's, I lifted a few things outside the budget. For Bonita, a denim smocked top; for Margaret, a floral prairie skirt with a flounce. They smiled when I brought them the items. And they rarely smiled. But it was the hat for James that got me in trouble. "Oh, give me a break," I said to the security guard, who followed me outside Bamberger's main door. I knew I could talk my way out of his accusation. "A dusty fedora? Small potatoes."

"Small?" he said, lifting a pinky finger to signify small. "When you add it all up? Last week? When I pointed to my eye? Like, I'm watching you?"

"That's what that meant?"

The police called it black-and-white theft. They had black-and-white videotape. And Greystone Park, too, called it black and white, although to me, when it came to people's lives you couldn't always believe what you saw. You couldn't see their minds. To me, taking items from Bamberger's was a sane response to an unjust, if not insane, world.

"So, what's going to burn this month?" Mike asked, as he walked by my front desk. A former employee of the Housing Authority, Mike Mullins was the AWAPS rehabilitation specialist. He didn't look like a specialist, but especially gave no hint of being a rehabilitator.

He was gaunt and hunkered over, though he never complained of back pain. He complained about the handling of the hostage crisis. *Day 302*, he'd say. *Day 325*. He complained about the price of gas and cigarettes, the high price of a wife and two children. In sum, he complained the world was beyond rehabilitation, so why bother. His job was to work with scofflaw landlords and aid them in fixing up their property. The thinking was, if their properties were in good shape the owners wouldn't be inclined to torch them.

"I haven't put it all together yet," I said.

"Atta' girl," Mike said, and walked away to his small office behind a makeshift half wall where he drank coffee and read the *New Haven Register* and *Fishing Life*. He used to smoke, too, until I complained to the chief that I couldn't breathe let alone do my work. After that, he left his desk every twenty minutes to smoke in the hall, or outside, or by the downstairs snack bar where he bought all his coffee. When he was through complaining, smoking, reading, drinking, he went home.

The AWAPS model was based on predictions—the ability to predict what pieces of property were likely to be torched. The chief called these predictors *variables* and I called them *variables* too. To be an arson risk, to end up on my *At-Risk List*, a house had to have three or four variables: liens, unpaid taxes, housing code violations, and previous fires.

I pored through big city books to see what houses had liens against them. I looked at lists of houses with unpaid taxes. I checked printouts of houses with code violations. I read data sheets of houses that had fires, even small fires. At the end of the month I would come up with my list. I couldn't say when a property might burn. Just that it could happen.

"Where are you with the *At-Risk List*?" asked the chief. He had just come back from lunch and stood at my desk.

"Almost done. Just double-checking the liens."

"Lean and mean," Mike called behind his half wall. We couldn't see him.

"Like you, Mike," the chief said. "Too much coffee and smokes."

"Esther's lean too," Mike called back.

"She's not mean, though. And she's slender through a clean life and hard work." My heart sang with "slender," which was the attractive version of thin. The chief winked at me. He had the kind of beautiful bald head on which you could live your entire life: You could pitch a tent on that head, plant a garden. It was a good-sized head with good color.

Behind the wall, we heard Mike's phone ring. "A-WAPS," he said. "Mike Mullins."

"I'd like to A-WAP him," whispered the chief. "I should have hired my son-in-law. He's an idiot too, but he doesn't sit still and he'd be out there working with these deadbeat landlords."

"Everyone would just scream nepotism," I whispered.

"Yeah," he said softly. "This way it's only me screaming."

I reveled in the fact that I was the good child. Mike, when he grew up, grew old, might eventually amount to something. But in the chief's mind, I'd always be the good one.

He clapped the flat of his hand on my desk, then walked away. "Whenever you have your list," he called out.

"Okay," I said back. I thought of how many times in my life I'd said *okay*. *Okay* was something I'd say even when I didn't hear the request or didn't have the slightest thought of fulfilling it. Most times after I said *okay*, I forgot what it was I was supposed to do. But for the chief, I'd be Johnny-on-the-spot.

"That was quick," he said when I put my hand-printed list on his desk. Once he looked it over, he would type up the list himself. He liked to say it was therapy. "You're busy concentrating on whole words or chunks of sentences. You don't have space in your brain to be thinking, *Oh, my daughter with her painful uterine cysts in Orlando*." I was flattered that he shared this. Cysts were personal. Uterine, more so. And in Orlando? I was family.

"Nice printing," he said to me, as he stared at my list. "Uh, oh," he said and slapped his hand on his desk. I waited, held my breath. "Here it is again!" I waited to be scolded, but instead he walked over to Mike's wall and yelled, even though he easily could have walked the three steps into Mike's cubby. "Mike! 539 Governor! It's been a four-variable for three months! Just a matter of time before Tucker torches it."

"I've tried the guy and tried the guy."

"Don't just try the guy. Get the guy. Get a detective. Track Tucker down and find out what's up. See if we can help him rectify 539."

"539 is a goner. Tucker is too far behind in arrears and violations."

"I just want it documented that we reached him."

"Okay boss."

The chief looked at me and hit his forehead with his fist.

I thought it best to leave the office. "I'm going to the Records Building," I said. "Start looking up properties for next month."

"No dragging her feet, this one here," the chief said loudly. "She means business."

"Meeny, miny, moe," Mike called.

"For the love of Christ," the chief whispered, and leaned heavily on my desk. "Meeny, miny, moe," he said in a shaky voice. Then he walked into his office. I heard the rolling wheels of his swivel chair. I heard the turning of the platen knob as he fed paper into his typewriter. And finally, the typing, which struck me as bombs hitting their target, showering the chief with sweet relief.

I picked up my shoulder purse and a legal pad and tiptoed out of office, trying not to call attention to myself. I didn't want the chief to hear more mouth from Mike. But in the silence of his laziness, Mike heard the door knob turn and called out, "Give 'em hell, kid."

On my way to research liens, I remembered that, in the mind of my mother, I was expecting. Six-weeks expectant. As I walked down Church Street, I imagined life forming and growing. I knew, almost for sure, my mother wouldn't throw me out if I was pregnant. If thrown, where would I go—where I wouldn't feel separate from myself?

The records office was on Orange Street, and the AWAPS office was on Church. I walked over there under a blazing summer sun, which in past weeks I ignored. In my work clothes, I made a point of disbelieving the true temperature. My brain sent a coded message to my body indicating that on work time I had to leave my body out of things. I was a head at work, albeit a pregnant head. The body I left at home.

But that was before I noticed Eddie Marcus in Traffic and Parking. The overhead florescent lights would shine down upon him and cast his face, his forearms, the curls on his head, in tawny brilliance. He was a calendar month: July.

Eddie's desk was positioned right by the main aisle, close to the door of the Assessor's Office, where I did my research. But that day, he wasn't at his desk, so I went to the bathroom to check myself in the mirror. I wasn't tawny or beautiful. But I was young, twenty-two, and sweaty, and this counted for something. My hair was wild with summer humidity, but it was uniformly wild—no hunks or strands breaking away from the pack. I left the bathroom, drank a Fanta from the soda machine, pinched my cheeks for color since the tomato heat flush was fading.

I walked back through Traffic and Parking and this time he was there. I walked by his desk, flipped my hair off my shoulder, and held my breath as if I were underwater. Even before I held my breath, I had trouble talking in air—he was truly that breathtaking. He looked like a perfect piece of fake fruit—a shimmering Golden Delicious with a Shirley Temple wig. If you like that look. Which I did.

He didn't say anything, but he purposely followed me with his head. In fact, he turned his entire body to watch me enter the Assessor's Office. But when the office door closed, we were lost to each other. I made some weak effort to thumb through the giant Grantor/Grantee book to see what owners had liens against their property, but all I could focus on was the image of Eddie cast in florescent light. When I left the Assessor's, I looked for him but he was gone. Later in the day, I got a call from my friend Steve Picarello in Building Inspection—the office next to Traffic and Parking.

"Eddie Marcus wants to know who you are," Steve said. I knew Steve from Naugy High, where I was president and he was vice president of the Spanish Club. Except to elect officers in Spanish class, the club had no meetings or purpose and Steve and I carried out our responsibilities as required. "I told him who you were," Steve said, "so now he knows who you are."

"Who's he?"

"Eddie Marcus."

"No, but who is he?"

"He does traffic education. He educates traffic. No, but really, he educates crossing guards at schools. I know him a little."

"He wants to know who I am?"

"Yeah, but don't get known. Not if you don't want to get involved in his ex's baby."

"If X is a baby? What?"

"He and his ex-girlfriend broke up, but she's having a baby. Stay away from him."

"Who'd you tell him I was?"

"Esther Schlag."

"He still interested?"

"He liked the Esther part. And your hair. His father is a doctor."

"What else you tell him about me?" I kept my voice as low as I could. I wanted to appear professional. I was, I believed, professional.

"Smart girl, college, good mother. Father MIA."

"MIA. He'll think Vietnam."

"Don't mention Vietnam," Mike Who Heard Everything said.

"Gotta go, Steve."

"Vaya con Dios," he said. "And let it go with Eddie."

Maybe it was Steve I really liked. He knew me when I was sixteen, when I couldn't imagine leaving my mother—not for college, or work, or any life event. I liked Steve well enough to show him photos of my father. "He looks normal here," he said. My mother sometimes invited Steve to dinner but he would look beyond her and say, as someone who seeks an exemption on religious grounds, that his mother was "making sauce." My mother and I understood this, knew, as fatherless Jews, we were excluded from Steve's life, his big family—four sisters, one brother, and a live-in grandma. I'd watch Steve walk away from our house, walk down the street holding his Spanish and world history books, and wish he'd invite my mother and me for sauce. "Please," I'd whisper.

After Steve made our introductions, I often ran into Eddie. I didn't so much run into him as ran at him, hoping to see and be seen. I'd walk through Traffic and Parking as often as I could, looking for him at his desk. I walked a path: down that main aisle to the Assessor's Office and then back again through the main aisle of Traffic and Parking to the bathroom, then to the soda machine, then back to the main aisle to the Assessor's, then back again to the bathroom. To convey I was working, I carried my yellow pad and looked irritated, as one might look if she had to repeatedly interrupt looking up liens in order to go to the bathroom.

One day, I passed him by the soda machine, but I didn't smile and he didn't smile either.

And one time, a guy whose desk was behind Eddie's spoke to me as I passed by: "He's training," the guy said. Whatever that meant. Eddie wasn't at his desk; that's all I knew. I didn't know who the guy was or who Eddie was or, for that matter, who I was or who I was to Eddie. Nevertheless, I had the impression I was starting to be something.

And I very much wanted to start something. My last boyfriend had been three years ago, back in college. I loved him until, before my eyes, he grew too orthodox for my taste. He prayed on the Coney Island roller coaster, when we hiked a ledge on Pike's Peak, before and after we ate. He became the very thing he'd once mocked. Prayer on a roller coaster? Couldn't he just scream?

Over the next week, Eddie began looking up as I passed by, as though *he* was the town assessor, appraising my worth, noting if I had sufficient luster. Finally, as I walked by his desk, he looked up and spoke. "*I say hip*," he said.

Hip, I thought. From "Rapper's Delight," one of the first rap songs way back. *I said a hip hop.* I danced a little over to the Grantor/Grantee index. Hip was not lost on me. I drew it in like the orange Fantas I'd been consuming. That he had a pregnant girlfriend made him neither more or less appealing. Maybe more. A pregnant girlfriend. Maybe he could do the same for me—make me an honest woman.

When I'd held out as long as I could in the Assessor's Office, I left and walked by his desk. He kept his head down, his curls waving a bit from the stand-up fan in the aisle. But I heard him: "*Hop*."

Hop. I sucked on it, like hard candy.

After two weeks of our pregnancy moratorium, my mother wanted me to make a statement. We'd been in our suspended wait-and-see period, and in that time I was waiting to see how I could extricate myself from the whole business. But I couldn't find a way.

"So, what's the story?" she asked, one evening at dinner. We were eating on the porch again, which required we wear sunglasses, both of us now wearing them. We picked at our salad nicoise.

I looked down at an imposing, dry mound of tuna.

"The pregnancy. Are you?"

"I am."

"So, what next?"

"Let's wait and see," I said.

"We already did that." With her sunglasses on, I couldn't read her, but I heard her: I was another disappointment, my father's daughter. I switched the subject to *my* big disappointment: "Is Armand ready to move in?"

"Don't worry about Armand."

It was hard not to worry about Armand. He was burly, as they used to say in the eighties. My mother might have liked burly—big. Big belt buckle, a big turquoise ring, a black Casio watch emblazoned with *G-Shock*. Too close, for my daughterly comfort, to G-Spot. Worse, but not really, heating and cooling had given him special insights into race relations, gun control, dogs versus cats, hot versus spicy. If he lived here, if he used my bedroom as an emporium for condenser coils and refrigerants, I was going to have twins.

"You're going to have the baby?"

"If all goes according to plan."

"What plan?

"To have the baby."

"You have a doctor?"

I moved salad around on my plate, making the lettuce overtake a black olive.

"Yes. In New Haven."

"What's his name?"

"Marcus." I said. Steve had said Eddie's father was a doctor.

"Dr. Marcus?"

"Yes."

She was making it worse. Couldn't she just hear a name and make peace with it? "Dr. Marcus on Sherman Avenue?"

"I think it's Sherman."

"Oh, my God, he's the herb and prayer doctor that Lena San Angelo sees. She swears by him. She goes to him for female problems and arthritis. He gives her some herbs and says a prayer and she swears by him."

"That's good to hear."

"Is he following you carefully? I mean, is he nutty?"

"No, he seems like a good guy."

"What does he say?"

"I'm in good health."

"About the baby and your not being married and living here."

"He says, 'Think only of life, new life. Believe in life and everything will work out.'"

"Hm," she said. She cut up her iceberg with a steak knife so all her pieces of lettuce were the size of spaghetti strands. "He's supposed to be a learned man."

"He seems like it."

"Well, okay, hon." She took a small mound of mayonnaise and put it on the side of her plate. "I shouldn't," she said, "but the tuna is a little dry."

"But it's good, Mom. A good salad nicoise. And everything will be okay. I'm sorry I'm putting you through a hardship."

She took off her sunglasses then, and I could see she was all teared up. Like she was overcome with a sudden insight and wanted me to see. "We must never think of a baby as a burden. Marcus is right. Let's just believe in life."

I took her hand and there we were, joined in the way we used to be. With my free hand, I reached for the mayo and put a dollop on my plate, too. "We agree," she said, watching me. "It is a little dry."

. . .

Weights and Measures was in the office next to AWAPS. Strictly speaking, Weights and Measures wasn't a next-door office—it was actually in the same room as AWAPS, with only a partial partition, four-feet high, dividing us. Originally, I wondered if the scales and weights were part of my job, if I was supposed to weigh evidence or measure some sort of arson substance or material. "Nothing to do with us. Don't worry about the scales," the chief said. Then some city workers came in, tore down the partition, and put in a floor-to-ceiling wall, which they then spackled and painted. "Now you're officially separated," said a man, who smiled and winked at me.

Not that Weights and Measures ever bothered me in the first place. The office seemed to be a non-office, the workers rarely there. Occasionally, before the wall, I saw an elderly man or an elderly woman come in. They'd do a little weighing and measuring, then leave.

The new wall was useful. The chief and I used the wall to tack up notices and flyers about housing rehab conferences or home energy savings programs. We pinned up a huge poster, ARSON KILLS, a red-and-black angry graphic, that faced my desk. There was a thank-you note from the mayor, thanking AWAPS for our contribution in restoring life to 462 Lambert Street, a near-dead, abandoned eyesore, which my variables flagged as an arson target. Mike saw the deadbeat landlord in the dog license office and asked if he wanted rehab money from the city. The guy did, he got the property cleaned up, and I took him off the *At-Risk List*. "Teamwork," Mike said.

"That's a stretch," the chief said. "Good thing the deadbeat has a dog. Otherwise, you'd never have contacted him."

"There's where you're wrong. I tried the guy. He just never returned the call."

"You tried. I tried. I tried to retire, but they kept me here for this new adventure in arson. Esther, promise me you'll stick around for a while. I need a good right hand."

I was his right hand, his front person. I sat at my desk, in the front of the office, and received visitors and directed them to the chief or Mike. When I could, I answered the questions and I always conducted myself in a manner I considered professional, cordial, and flirtatious.

Men in dark suits and sunglasses often came in and asked to see the chief. Always they were blanketed—head to shoe—in overbearing perfume: a cover, of course, for their lunch sex. "May I tell him who you folks are?"

"Yes, please. Tell him detectives Michaels and Dunn."

We were a small operation. There was no intercom. I could have sent them the five steps it took to reach the chief's office, but I liked to play executive protector. I walked down to the chief's office. "Detectives Michaels and Dunn are here to see you."

"Thanks, Esther. Send them in."

"He's straight ahead and waiting for you." I gave them a big smile even though they scared me. They created a big wind just by lifting up their leather-bound notebooks. They walked by me with their summer blazers, their pistols, their belt buckles the size of their pistols, their sweet smells of Aqua Velva and Listerine. Who did they think they were fooling?

"Any word on Hippolitis?" the chief asked. The men made a lot of noise rearranging chairs and dropping their leather notebooks on the brown conference table. If there wasn't indoor-outdoor carpeting it would have sounded like a brawl in there.

"Hippolitis went down with his building. Dumb guy was a loser with an accelerant," either Michaels or Dunn said. "Torched so badly you couldn't tell if it was man or pig." I heard the chief's light step, his thick Hush Puppies, as he got up to close the door. I knew he wanted to save me from the details but I already heard.

Eddie walked in just then, and I nearly fell off my chair. "Is this Weights and Measures?"

"It's AWAPS."

"You're Esther."

"Weights and Measures are on other side of the wall," I said. "You have something to measure?"

"I don't need to measure. I already know."

"I wouldn't touch that line," I said. As we used to say. I looked down at my pink *While You Were Away* pad and wrote "*Eddie was here*," as a kind of warning.

Still, I agreed to go to dinner with him. Under the overhead lights here he didn't look like fake fruit; not say like a burnished pear in a fake fruit arrangement. There was a little sweat on his forehead which made him more like actual fruit—a wedge of ripe cantaloupe, a slice of watermelon. *Wet fruit*, my mother called it. As opposed to a dried raisin or a fig.

Over rigatoni, he was quiet. "Always good," he said of his food. I wanted to put him on a scale to see what I had here. How many dust particles per cubic volume of space his words added up to. Look at me, I wanted to say. Shy, I thought. Shy! I tried drawing him out. I asked about his job. He mentioned crossing guards by name as if I knew them: "Marilyn," "Gloria." Did he believe I knew people I didn't know? When I gently pressed, he came back with, "Marilyn Distephano? Gloria Sparks?"

"Yes?" I asked. Waiting for more. But there was no more except another mouthful of red clam sauce over his pasta. After another glass of wine, however, he opened up—about the very subject I wanted to know more. Pregnant Barbara Ann, his ex-girlfriend.

"Everything's got to be about her," he said. "Barbara Ann's apartment, Barbara Ann's sofa, Barbara Ann's baby shower. It's my baby too."

I felt bad for him and this fact made me also open up—about living with my mother and about my job and the variables, the *At-Risk List*. Maybe I made myself sound more important than I was. Maybe I was important. I hadn't made up my mind about myself.

"So, what's tops on your list?" he asked me. "What's gonna burn?"

"539 Governor Street."

"539 Governor?"

I didn't like that the address drew what seemed to be interest and recognition. I thought he'd just nod and be impressed that I had inside information.

"I know that guy," he said.

"Maybe I have the wrong address."

"No, I think you got the right guy."

"He's not my guy."

"No, no. He's your guy. He'd torch it. I've known 539 all my life. I grew up here, you know. His place is a wreck. Yeah, I can definitely see him torching it. He cares shit about his tenants. I'll tell him you're watching. Right? You watch the place?"

"No, no. I just make a list. I don't come to his house and arrest him."

"Esther. I don't know you, Esther, but I think you're underestimating yourself."

"No. Don't say anything until I check the address."

That's all I needed. To blow this job. My heart was all revved up, and I tried calming myself. He was likely lying about his friend. What were the odds his friend was 539? He was that kind of practically gorgeous guy who lies in order to get girls in bed. Besides, he was probably not desirable these days: a guy whose ex is pregnant? Who'd want him?

"Let's change the subject," he said. "You like living in Naugatuck? Isn't that the town that used to smell?"

"It used to stink," I said. "From the rubber company. And the river. But it cleaned itself up."

A con man trying to play me for his own deceptive pleasure. Barbara Ann was likely pregnant with someone else's baby, his father not even a doctor.

"Is your father the herb doctor? My mother's friend sees him. She says he prays for her and she gets better."

"Yep. Herbs and prayer. He's the best. Wanna meet him?"

"No, I was just asking."

"Come on. I practically put him to bed every night. He won't stop reading and working. Come on." He paid the check, took my hand, led me out the door. His hand was warm, but maybe it had to do with the evening. A hot July evening, the streets still light. In parts of the city, fires were in their infancy, or on the brink of being conceived.

"I'm a daddy's boy," he said. "You should know that about me."

"I'm a momma's girl," I said. Right, I thought. We are just two peas in a pod.

The night was hot, but Eddie had the windows down and the wind was racing across my knees. My denim skirt rose up high on my thighs and I made no effort to yank it down. No use: jean skirts have a mind of their own.

"I'm going to be a good father," he said. I didn't want to think of him as a father. In fact, I tried to have no thoughts. Except 539, which was still there, growing bigger in my mind.

His father's medical office was in a regular city neighborhood: two-story houses lined both sides of the street and Dr. Marcus's office was wedged right in there, a modest two-story with no signage I could see. Eddie pointed to the house next door. "That's his actual house, but my mother kicks him out half the time."

We knocked on the doctor's first-floor door and waited. I stood behind Eddie and wondered how he would introduce me. I didn't know how to introduce me.

As it turned out, I needn't have worried about being introduced or even seen. The father, a small, frail man, only had eyes for Eddie. He looked up at Eddie with frail adoration. He hooked an arm around Eddie's neck, brought him close and hugged him. "How you doing, son? How's Barbara Ann?"

No secrets in this family.

"Barbara Ann is Barbara Ann," Eddie said, which was what I might have said if I was in his position and trying to deny a major event that would forever change my life.

The bottom floor seemed to be a waiting room, and we climbed the stairs, me climbing behind Eddie. It wasn't until we walked into the father's office that I seemed to register with him. He gestured to two chairs next to his desk covered with stacks of papers. Two fans were going, and the papers were rustling but staying in place.

Eddie and I sat and Dr. Marcus stood, holding onto the edge of his desk. "And this young lady?" he asked.

"Esther," Eddie said.

"Queen Esther," his father said.

"In a way," I said.

Eddie sat next to me, and across from us Dr. Marcus sat down at his straight back desk chair. He looked to be in his seventies, more the age of Eddie's grandfather. Maybe Eddie was from a second marriage or adopted as an adult. An old doctor and his barren wife finally adopt a boy, a twenty-five-year-old city worker who trains school crossing guards.

"So, Queen Esther," Dr. Marcus went on. "Smart, brave, beautiful Queen Esther. You Jewish?"

"My father was German Jewish. So, yes, I guess I am. Not in a big way."

"Like a lot of Jews."

"How are you Dad?" Eddie asked. He leaned in close to his father. "You hot in here?"

"I got my fans. I got him." He pointed to the photo on his desk of the Maharishi. "This is who I pray to. But, you, Esther, talk to me."

"Hello," I said.

"Hello. So, you work with Eddie? You teach with Barbara Ann?"

"She works for AWAPS," Eddie said.

"A-WACS? You on leave?"

"Arson Warning and Prevention Strategy," I said slowly. "AWAPS."

"That's good," he said. "That's a very good thing. Too much arson. You're saving lives."

"I think so. But some guys die. Some landlord died by torching his own building."

Dr. Marcus put his hands over his ears. I put them over mine too. We were both appalled.

Eddie stood now with his hands in his pocket. He shuffled from foot to foot, watching his father and me. His father looked up at him, but then took my hand. "An unmarried son with a baby on the way. They won't marry, Esther. They are oil and water and they've made a baby. What do we do?"

"Pray," I said, looking at the Maharishi.

"You are so right," he said.

He turned a pole fan toward me, which I took to be a kind, gallant gesture, worthy of a doctor. He was wearing a white short-sleeved shirt, and altogether he looked white, pale, nearly not there. With the fan turned toward me, the papers on his desk were now flying, falling on the floor, but he didn't seem to care. He closed his eyes then, right in front of us.

"It's time for you to go home, Dad," Eddie said. "You're tired."

His father looked through his office window to the window next door, the window of his own house, where apparently he'd been banished. He sighed and lifted his shoulders in an *it's no use* shrug. "I'll sleep here tonight." He looked at me intently, as though evaluating me for the appropriate herbs. "You seem like a smart girl," he said.

"I have to take Esther to her car. She lives in Naugatuck with her mother." He gave his father a big hug. "Don't stay up too late, Dad."

His father stood then and weakly hit Eddie's back in a gesture of you're a loveable, derelict son who's gotten himself into a messy situation with one woman and now you're with another woman, so watch yourself.

"Goodnight. And watch yourself," he said to Eddie.

"And you?" he said to me. He stared at me with an expression, patient and expectant. He opened his eyes wide. I didn't know what to say. How could I answer something if I didn't know the question?

"I hope you can sleep in this heat," I said to him finally.

"I hope you can, too," he said. He extended his hand and I took it. My grip was firmer than his, a whisper of a hand.

We walked to Eddie's car.

"So, where to?" he asked.

He lived two blocks away, on Hurlburt. I lived with my mother four towns away and my car was still in the city parking lot downtown. His apartment was the closest and he was standing very close to me, so close the belt buckle on his pleated slacks pressed tight against my stomach.

"Where to?" Eddie asked again. He started brushing some strands away from the crown of my head, down to the top of my neck. "To my car," I said. When his finger got stuck on a snarl, he didn't pull it, but chose another strand, a section with no snags or snarls. He seemed to find his way easily. "My mother is waiting up for me," I said.

"Yo automobile. She want to be ridin' in her automobile."

Funny, last time I looked he was white. He'd gone hip hop on me, playing some character he'd made up.

"That's nice," he said. "You should go home and see yo momma." He said this, but he continued running his fingertips through the top part of my hair.

"Yes, I'm going to go home," I said.

"You know I was just busting on you. About 539. I don't know the guy."

"I figured."

"I'd had a little wine. And you were cute talking about your variables."

"Not very nice."

"Let me make it up to you."

His cologne was getting to me. Killing me, in a way neither all good nor all bad.

"Oh, no. No, no."

"No? I have a new ceiling fan that creates a big breeze, like air conditioning. I have ice cold sodas. I won't ever bust on you again. That was bad. I'm sorry, Esther. My father likes you. I like you." He ran his finger down the side of my face. "Come with me."

His belt buckle was radiating heat.

He was stroking my forehead now with one finger, going from my eyebrow all the way back behind my head. I stood still and let myself be touched. My body was buzzing.

"Soda?" I said.

"Lots and lots of soda. All kinds."

"Okay. I'll have a soda before I go home."

Eddie cupped the back of my head with his hand and directed me toward his car. He opened the door for me and then walked around to his own side. I was diminishing. I was less than I was and growing smaller.

He started down the street, down Sherman, and took a left on Whalley. I knew in a minute we'd be close to his place. The windows in his car were open but the heat was torturing me. My jean skirt was letting hot air up my legs and trapping it there. Between my thighs, I saw a burrow of sweat. All I wanted was an ice-cold soda. That's all I wanted. To pour it over my head, splash it on my legs.

It was dark now, but the streetlights were bright and I saw coming toward us, coming from downtown, a Crown Victoria. It was big and fierce, moving slowly, like a cruising fish, a barracuda. A white light, a dome light, shone down on a passenger, an older woman, who was applying lipstick. The car slowed for traffic and I stared at her. I'd seen her face in a photo. She was the chief's wife. I was sure of it. And a second before the dome light went off, I was sure I identified the driver as the chief. They might have been returning home after a late evening nightcap or a movie.

The sweat between my thighs had become a watering trough. Water bubbled on my knees.

"Can you pull over?" I asked Eddie.

"Pull over?"

"I feel sick."

"Sick? The rigatoni?"

"No. I know what it is. I didn't want to tell you because of Barbara Ann."

"What? No. What?"

"Two-months expecting."

"No. Esther."

"You have enough problems. I didn't want to say anything."

"Esther," he said again, and beyond that nothing—probably a guy who's used to bad news. He pulled over, stopped, pointed to a bar with a florescent green shamrock in the window. "Ladies room in the back," he said.

I pretended to go for the bar, but then ran in the direction of the Crown Vic. The car was going south, toward Westville, where the grown-ups live.

I ran down Whalley, passing a grocery, a gas station, a money exchange store. Running cooled me off, the night air combined with my freedom. There were a series of traffic lights ahead. Maybe the lights would be with me. Or not. I couldn't tell where the car was now. In the dark, all the cars looked like big, dark cruisers, all Crown Vics. But one car out there was the right one. And believing this, I ran fast and hard, my feet, in my leather sandals, pounding the sidewalk. I hoped I could be heard. But even if no one heard me, even if the dark, thick air created an impenetrable barrier, I screamed anyway—"Chief! Chief!"

As in Life

WHEN I WALK through the door of Schmurr's, the lights are dim and flat, and hanging from round racks, the women's sweatshirts look exhausted. Outside it's raining hard, and I set my wet umbrella in the dark alcove near the front door. On one side of the alcove, bordering the stairs to the second floor, baby clothes hang from a high pole. Occasionally, like now, toward Christmas, a customer might buy an infant gown or a one-piece romper. But otherwise, the baby clothes live here like curled-up bats, sleeping.

On the first floor of Schmurr's, lots of clothes sleep: khaki slacks with elastic waists, embroidered cardigans, robe and nightie sets. Stuart's real bread and butter comes from the Catholic school uniforms on the second floor. But the first floor lives on—two long aisles like two underground tunnels—for parents who, in the course of buying clothes for their children, have an arresting impulse to buy for themselves something they didn't know they needed.

Schmurr's used to sell it all and sell it like crazy and our slogan for the past seven decades was, "This, that, the whole Schmurr." This was when the U.S. Rubber Company, Naugatuck Footwear Division, was our neighbor across the street. Before U.S. Rubber closed shop, the rubber workers would rush in on their breaks looking for thermal tees, Playtex bras, Queen Casual pantsuits. My father, his yellow measuring tape hanging from his neck like a second tie, was The Schmurr then. Mr. Irving Schmurr. Now the Schmurr in charge is my brother, Stuart, and he stays afloat by outfitting the children of Blessed Sacrament, Saint Hedwig's, Our Lady of Mount Carmel.

Though the store looks closed, it's only noon and I know Stuart is alone, or perhaps with a single customer upstairs. I start up the steps where a bit of light shines down from the second level. On the landing, Stuart has set a bunch of empty boxes, not yet broken down. I climb over some and make for the second set of stairs, looking ahead for light. And there is light, but not much. To keep this store fully lit costs more than Stuart can afford.

He's waiting for me at the top of the stairs, a grin on his face. "Thanks for coming," he says. He's holding a box in his hands, and though I know it's ludicrous I think he has a present for me. My heart lifts and I walk up faster, ready to receive it.

"He nearly kicked yesterday," he says, referring to our ninety-year-old father. I stop halfway up the second set of stairs to hear the story through. "He told the physical therapist she had no business working if she's pregnant. Then he told an aide she had no business working when she has a cold. Then he called in the head dietician to tell her the food stinks. After that, he fell asleep."

Stuart puts the box under his arm, like it's a football. He will always look like the athlete he formerly was. "So, he sleeps right through dinner and Mom and I can't wake him. But he comes out of it at ten and asks for a piece of fish! And they give him fish! A piece of scrod! What, he thinks he's on a Carnival Cruise? What is this, the Love Boat?"

Only my father can score scrod at ten at Harbor View Nursing Home. This is because they're scared of him. "You see a harbor here?" he asks the staff. "There's no harbor here. You got to travel fifty miles to get a harbor view and that harbor smells like piss. Just like here. Piss View, you could call it." When he is not insulting anyone, his mind is dull. But when he wants to trip you up, he's sharp as a tack. But the staff shot back. They sent him home today, and now he's our problem.

When I reach the top of the stairs, I see Stuart's box is empty—a box previously so full of promise and now it's empty. What would I have wanted? I could use a new winter coat, leather with vintage buttons. Either that, or my marriage back, but Stuart can't give me that either. "El," he says, holding the box over his head. "Ever hear of the Colorado Avalanche?"

"Basketball?"

"Hockey."

"They good?"

"Like this."

He throws the box down yelling, "Av . . . a . . . lanche," trying to make his voice go from boom to poof, simulating a boulder falling into a far-away canyon. I'd like to say we only act this stupid with each other, but the truth is we act stupid together and apart. It's in our stupid Schmurr blood. The box lands on the others, bounces a bit, and knocks another box down the steps. "What if there's a customer?" I ask.

"You nuts?"

I walk into the open space of the second floor and see what I always see: gray linoleum, wallpaper printed with brown air balloons, and, attached to the outside of the dressing room, the three-paneled mirror where I watched myself grow up. Where my father used to fit the former mayor and rubber executives for sport coats; the rubber workers for their wedding suits and church slacks. The former mayor was jailed, re-elected, then died. The rubber factory moved away and the Naugatuck rubber workers took office jobs in Waterbury or line jobs on the other side of town, where they made lipstick tubes and safety pins. Schmurr's former sales girls—Lena, Theresa, Esther, Martha, Barbara, Rita—have all died or fallen into unremitting disrepair.

But here on the second floor of Schmurr's Department Store, Poll Parrot Shoes will always live on, in good health, in a good home, in the back room. Stuart long ago got rid of the tiny shoe department, but even so, the blue parrot still perches on an invisible twig in the display window of the former shoe section. Below the blue parrot, where the seven aqua-covered seats and the fitting stool used to be, sits a 1930s Singer sewing machine. Schmurr's long-time tailor, evicted from his own father's long-time tailor shop, now offers in-house tailoring from his ancient sewing setup. Behind his worn wood counter, Anthony, the son of Anthony, alters the Catholic blazers, the occasional suit for a communion, wedding, burial.

Stuart goes behind a glass-topped counter where he's set a big carton of child-sized skirts, navy skirts with big box pleats. The carton is wet from the rain, although the small skirts are folded in plastic that keeps them dry and safe. Stuart is also wet from helping the UPS man unload the truck. His forehead, always smooth with good color, is damp, and so is his sporty striped knit jersey. He picks up a bunch of the wrapped skirts and throws them into four piles—small, medium, large, extra-large. "We need you here," he says. "Mom should be able to hire full-time help in a few days and then you can head back to New London. Dad can't walk and he's down to 115 pounds."

"I dropped the kids with Seth and I can't stay a full week but I can help interview a live-in. I have a low case load at work and no one's in crisis."

"Even two, three days would be great. I can go there after work and help him go to the bathroom and get ready for bed, but that's it. If I stay longer, he'll yell at me. He never lets up; it's always I have too much stock and not enough help. I can't afford help."

"I know. I know."

We stand there for a moment not saying anything, just happy to be sad with each other. I love my brother. What would we do alone? "I can't believe they sent him home," I say.

"He insulted everyone. It was time to move on. Last night he says to the aide, 'I'm sitting here alone for hours and you're out there talking to some guy with a fat ass.'"

Our father was born without a fine mesh strainer, and as a result anything that comes into his brain, any disturbing or anxious or mean thought, goes directly into his mouth exactly as it's been delivered to him from his circuits. He doesn't have the cognitive wherewithal to be diplomatic or euphemize. He's been doing this to Stuart and me all our lives; to my mother, all her married life. We'd like to euthanize him.

I look around and notice Stuart has a new display of fleece-lined jackets. He buys anything that goes with the Catholic school uniform; anything the uniform wearer would wear when the uniform comes off; and anything that goes over and under the uniforms. Except for bras. That would require a female salesclerk to help with fitting. And he can't afford to hire *a good woman*, as my mother would say.

I see a thick, gray hooded sweatshirt, bright in this one section of overhead light, and I think of buying one for Seth, but we're separated and I'm not sure of the appropriateness of a clothing gift.

Stuart takes the now-empty carton of skirts, carries it to the top of the stairs and calls out: Anyone down there? He waits a few seconds and hurls the wet carton down to the landing, where it lands on other cartons. It makes the groaning sound of a man being belly punched, and from the landing we hear the muffled hush and scuff of footsteps followed by the hoarse voice of Anthony. "Hey. You trying to kill me?"

Not on your life. Stuart needs Anthony. Now, killing our father; well, killing our father is a different matter. We would rather he not die; we would rather he be different—rational, kind, appreciative of my mother's heroic efforts to keep him alive. But since this will never happen in our lifetime, we would like to shorten his. Or so we like to say—Stuart and I. In traumatic times, talking this way keeps our spirits high.

I say good-bye to Stuart and Anthony. Together, they keep Schmurr's afloat, though often Anthony is sewing, which leaves Stuart alone to run two floors of a store that may itself decide, some day soon, not to get up one morning.

In the car, I have to shove aside my dog, who wants to drive. The rain has let up; the sun is starting to strain through and I am so grateful. So grateful for a bit of sun. I am light dependent. I get depressed on dark days and in the dark. Now that it's winter, I put on my pajamas after seven in the evening because I know I'm finished—no light, no nothing. I had nothing for Seth after seven. He had nothing for me before seven. Eventually, neither of us had nothing for the other, anytime.

Rags has her white head in my lap as I drive up the hill to my parents' house. If my father dies while I'm here, I'll need my dog. Besides, I don't want to leave her alone in Seth's apartment while he's at work, the girls at school. She won't know where she is.

Going up Millville Avenue in my Caprice, I am reminded of my recurring dream of driving up Millville Avenue in my Caprice. The Caprice in my dream can barely make it up the hill; the power or juice has dried up and my car is at an extreme slant—meaning it's nearly vertical, the hood like a horse rearing up, its snout in the air. I am alone in a car that's tipping backward, hood first—almost like my father, although he's been falling forward.

His last fall, face first onto the bathroom floor, was the fall that split his nose. My mother found him and called the ambulance. He was ninety; we thought this was it. In the ER, on a hard pallet, he lay for hours and peed in the pants of a four-piece ensemble he'd worn every day since World War II. Not the same suit of clothes, but always four pieces: dress shirt, dress pants, vest, jacket. And tie. Five pieces really. He wore all five pieces in the winter because he was cold; he wore all five pieces in the summer because he was cold. For the past eight months, he wore all five pieces at night, too. He wouldn't take them off. We thought he wanted to die wearing all five pieces. We could only guess he wanted it said: in death, as in life, he was a gentleman. He was almost there; the words almost spoken.

But from the ER he went to acute care, where they told him he had congestive heart failure and he had to take off his suit. They put him in a gown, a white hospital gown with blue dots, and it must have been then and there, in acute care, that he vowed if he wasn't going to die in his five-piece suit he wasn't going to die at all.

From acute care, he was sent to a nursing home for rehab. Rehab! We thought. Right. Rehab. "Rehab?" Stuart had said, looking puzzled. "I guess it's better than saying, 'Hospice.'"

My mother said, "Good. He'll gain some weight; he won't look so bad when he dies."

We didn't think he'd last a week. But for rehab we dressed him in a jog outfit and he must have been dead serious about staying alive in a jog suit because he didn't die. In rehab things went from worse to better; he was, at ninety, rehabbed; and as a rehabbed, dying man he was sent home.

Rags recognizes this home—my parents' aqua ranch. She must think to herself, *aqua ranch, bone on rug.* This is because my mother, in anticipation of a visit by Rags, always leaves, beside her kitchen chair, a bone or a cookie on a small cotton mat. And here is Rags, eating her bone-shaped cookie on a simulated Persian scatter rug. As she works on the cookie, pieces fall out of her mouth and she stares at them with steadfast anticipation—guarding every tiny bit she has coming to her.

"I almost lost him yesterday," my mother says, sitting in her cushioned kitchen chair. "We couldn't wake him up at the home. Stuart kept yelling, 'Dad, dinner. Dad. Dad.' I felt sorry for him. For Stuart. Seeing his father that way."

"I heard Dad got tired insulting everyone."

"He got tired, but they got more tired. Now I'm tired. I'm exhausted, Ellen. And we need to hire a live-in. The home said so and I know so. I can't handle him here alone. If I fall with him, that's it. We'll both end up in homes." She pauses and re-settles herself into the back cushion of her chair. She's quiet as she never is, and I imagine her imagining herself falling with him, the two of them side-by-side on the bathroom floor. The closest they've been in years.

"Look at her mopping up every last crumb," my mother says of Rags. You couldn't mistake my mother for anything other than a mother. I adore her down to her bent bones, her balding head, her stretch pants and smock top. She has that mother style—the colorless formerly green eyes that fall and rest on you as though you're a weary traveler, the prodigal daughter come home after living twenty years in an inactive volcano in the Yucatan. I may look like I've lived in an inactive volcano; I may look like I've smoked pot daily for twenty years, but really I just need my hair straightened and the gray toned down.

"Is he awake now?" I ask.

"Yeah, go see him. He's in the den."

I'm in no great rush. I'm afraid to see him. I've always been afraid of him. And now that he's frail and has received a reprieve from dying, I'm still afraid of him. The customers at Schmurr's loved him, the town loved him, he sat on the Finance Board for forty years. He was Naugatuck's Man of the Year five times and even when he wasn't Man of the Year he was man of the year. My fear of him is that he'll yell at me. Since I was born, I was the child who needed perpetual improvement. *Don't slump! Don't whine! Be on time! Exercise! You're too thin! Why'd you get a B in gym?! Why's your hair frizzy? Be a blond! Don't be a slob! Don't say, "ya know." Get your taxes in! Eat with gusto!*

"Rags, you pig, come on," I say. "We'll say hi to Grandpa."

We go to say hi, but stop at the den door.

I say the *Shema*. I don't know what else to say and I don't think the *Shema* is the right prayer, but I know you can say it to mark parts of the day, especially the passing of day into night. So I say it in the barest whisper, then knock softly on the door and walk in.

He's sitting in his rocker, a 1970s Hitchcock with the faux-Colonial pad on the seat and back. He's sat in that rocker for thirty years; listened to daily dirty jokes from his stockbroker in that chair; watched 1 million football games and 54,050 re-reruns of Perry Mason; told my mother 94,060 times that she had a fat ass; told her 206,876 times that in her eyes he does nothing right; drank 109,080 cups of decaf;

considered 2,056 times that maybe he was wrong to buy on margin; worried 900,000 times that he should have sold Aetna higher and Pfizer later. To have lost so much. In that chair, he always wore his five-piece suit; later, his five-piece, food-stained suit. He still sits in that chair, hoping to hit it big, even though he looks now like a white goat, dying in a gray jog outfit.

He barely looks up when I come in. Rags walks over to him, her tail wagging, not realizing he is mean and dying and worrying about his falling financial empire and Schmurr's overstocks. He doesn't pat her, but says to her, "Rags." To me he says with his eyes closed, "I don't know where I'm at."

"You're home. Harbor View said you were ready to go."

"Go where?"

"Here."

"Where am I?"

"Here, Dad. At your house." I'm standing in front of him; my only other choice for seating is the hospital bed. I don't think I can sit on the bed because he always yelled at Stuart and me if we sat on our beds. "No sitting on beds!" he'd yell. "You want to sit? Sit in a chair!" Beds were for sleeping. You can nap on the bed, he'd said, or sleep. But in his troubled mind, if you sat on the bed, you'd wrinkle the spread. You'd leave a crater. The bed, for the rest of its life, would have a crater memory it couldn't forget or smooth over.

"I'm telling you," he says, his voice too weak to rise and register wrath. "I don't know where I'm at."

"Tell me what you mean."

"Money. I need to talk to Elliot Rabinowitz."

"Elliot's gone, Dad. You mean Larry Levy."

"I didn't say Larry Levy, did I?" There is a murderous undertone in his voice and I try not to be afraid. "I said Elliot Rabinowitz." He sounds like he's growling, but he's really trying to clear his throat. "We have to hire live-in help," he says, "and I don't know where I'm at."

While fifty years ago my father looked dead while sleeping, he now looks dead while awake. His mouth is open at rest, his eyes are closed while talking. He puts his hands over his face, looks down, and clears his throat. He clears his throat so often I have discerned the different tones from his larynx. His voice resonates with ancient music from Central Asia. Tuvan and Tibetan peoples know an ancient form of song, throat singing, where words are replaced by soulful, throaty air blasts. I heard throat singers once with Seth before we were separated. He came home one night with tickets to a throat-singing concert. I wanted orchids and he knew it, but I got throat singers and, though I wouldn't tell Seth, I liked the throat people. Their music, their songs, were the sounds we all made as kids—imitating an old door being opened in an abandoned mansion. We liked the noises that came from down deep, our voices rich with guttural groans, and we opened those creaking doors over and over, testing what our bodies could do.

"It's Larry you want. He did your estate planning. He'll tell us." I speak above the throat sounds, using the noises as a bamboo screen to hide me.

He has stopped clearing his throat and looks at me. He is so old he's scary and I can barely look back at him. He is so white, I can barely see him. Could it happen now? Could he be ready to step off the curb and cross over? "You and mother have stopped listening to me. I didn't say Larry and you know I didn't!"

He takes his hands from his face and sets them in his lap. With one hand he begins rubbing the fingers of the other. He rubs one finger at a time, applying imaginary lotion. When he's feeling upbeat and alive, he'll pump real lotion from a tropical green dispenser emblazoned with hard-sell words: *painful, cracked, rash, burn.*

"I can't feel my fingers," he says, his eyes closed.

"I'm sorry."

"No, that part I'm used to. Wait, there's more. Come over and listen so I don't have to say it twice." He holds up his hands, and with his eyes closed he seems to wince and grimace as if he's calling upon his entire bodily reserve not to kill me.

He takes his index finger, points it at himself, and bends it over and over. Now, this could be the gesture of a man pointing a gun at his head and repeatedly pulling the trigger. Or it could be Captain Hook trying to summon me with a crooked, creamed finger. In reality, if the real Captain Hook was beckoning me, I could run off the boat and live off forest chokeberries. But if Captain Hook is my father, I am obliged to move closer. So, I move closer. I move so close I see the moons on the captain's head, the seas of the moon, even the view of earth. I see on earth, a father seated in a rocker and a small girl standing before him, peeing in her pants.

"Closer," he says. I take a step closer, terrified, and look down.

"I said, 'Elliot Rabinowitz.'"

"I'll call," I say.

"Good," he says. "Tell him I want to hire live-in help and I want to deduct it from my income tax."

"Okay, Dad." I turn around and start walking out of his den.

"Ellen. Wait."

"Yep," I say, waiting. I half turn, my own arthritis pain stopping me from a full turnaround.

"You're right." My heart sings. He's never told me I was right. I'm not sure what he's admitting to here, but I'll take it—his recognition that, in all of life, there is one thing I know that he doesn't. "Elliot's dead."

"Elliot's dead," I repeat.

"Long-time dead. I just remembered."

"I thought he might be dead," I say.

"He was a son-of-a-bitch. He made mistakes and couldn't add a simple row of figures. But I liked him. Call Larry if you want. At least he's alive."

"I'll call and ask him where you're at."

He doesn't answer and I take that to mean I'm dismissed. "I'll bring in your dinner later," I say. He still says nothing. And after my offer of dinner, I have nothing more to give him. "Rags," I say, and Rags comes. She lives for my commands, voice, smell. Seth, however, needs more from me. He needs deeper more private things that belong to me: my salty prosciutto, my warm artichoke hearts, and I'm unwilling to part with them. With two small kids and old parents, I have to keep something for myself.

My mother is in the kitchen looking at notes the nursing home gave her. "They gave me numbers to call for live-in help, but these places charge two hundred a day. Dad will never agree to that."

"We have to lie to him."

"He'll know. He still does the checkbook and scrutinizes every entry. I think it's time to call Mark Manuscz. Mark Manuscz's mother had a wonderful live-in Polish woman. Mark paid her under-the-table and said she was so reasonable. So much cheaper than a home. His mother loved that woman. She loved the woman so much that when his mother finally had to go to a home, Mark still hired the woman to come sit with her. She was like family."

Mark Manuscz is the last man alive I would call. In my present situation, calling Mark Manuscz is like calling a marriage undertaker.

When we were younger we called him Moose. He hasn't heard from me directly in fifteen years—the fifteen years I've been married. I live in New London, over an hour away, and he stayed here in Naugatuck. He's the local podiatrist and my first boyfriend. My first and only boyfriend in high school; my only lover during college breaks and summer vacations. He works my mother's feet and he works them hard, but he doesn't charge her. For me. In my memory.

In college, we didn't see each other during the school year, but if we were both home for Christmas, Thanksgiving, summer, we started right up again. "He's a little rough," my mother says. "A lot of women stopped going to him. The girls at the store, Theresa, Lena, Martha, Rita, they used to go see him. He hurts. But he's good."

I call Mark because he can tell me where to go for round-the-clock help. He can tell me, as he used to tell me, where to go for all kinds of things. To IHOP for pancakes; to Breen Field for tennis; to Yale Co-op for albums; to Andrew Mountain to kiss and touch each other. I hope

I don't have to reveal I'm separated; he'll tell me where to go for that and I don't want to go there.

"You have to call the Polish Place," he tells me. "They have the best live-ins. Don't even bother calling other agencies. The Polish Place. Here's the number. They get good women. They'll do anything, those women; they want to be part of the family. They'll cook, shop, sweet talk, change diapers."

"He won't write checks."

"They like to be paid under the table. Here's the number. You call and ask for Yvonna. Tell her I sent you. You around for a few days? Come see me for lunch. I know the best place."

I tell him I can't come to lunch and he says he'll come to me.

I know I'm cooked. He has always cooked me, heated me up like a progressive radiator coil. It was the seam on his pants. He had a rough inseam on his jeans which I still remember. I could fondle that seam and it sent me and him through the roof. The seam, rough and almost meaty, stood for something else. Finally we lived out its symbolism. But then I went off to college and fell in love with other inseams.

Since I still have the phone in my hands, I call Seth and the girls. Seth sounds as if he's speaking to me behind a locked door, as if he's taking the time to say a few words but has no desire to be heard. "How's your father?" he barely says.

Give me a break, Tight Throat, I want to say, but say instead, "Frail, old, and mean. How are you?"

"All right. You didn't pack their bathing suits and I can't take them to the Y."

"What else did I do wrong?"

"I won't get into that now. You want to talk to them?"

I am so mad at him. My father is dying and he won't give me a break. Jill comes to the phone. "Hi Mommy, is Grandpa still alive?"

"Yes, sweetie."

"Oh." She sounds a little disappointed. As though she hasn't had enough drama in her life, she needs her grandfather to die. "Daddy's mad we don't have our bathing suits. He's going to take us to J. C. Penney for bathing suits and buy us a cinnamon bun. You want to talk to Paula?"

Paula comes to the phone and sounds weary, depleted. "Hi Mom," she barely says. "Dad's mad again. You didn't pack our bathing suits and he wants to buy me a bathing suit and I only want a two-piece and he probably won't buy me one."

"It's just for swimming."

"It's just my self-esteem." For a twelve-year-old, she is a smart ass, but I would never say that to her face. When I was twelve, my father, face-to-face, and again and again, called me *pain-in-the-ass*. It was his way of expressing affection.

I can't seem to get a break anywhere. After dinner, I go outside to the back yard and because it's too cold and too wet I can only stand and look out over Hunter's Mountain, where from this back yard, I used to sit and stare. In my childhood dreams, I used to fly over Hunter's Mountain, over trees and telephone wires. Now in my dreams I fly either to escape people or to prove to them how powerful I am. Sometimes, however, I don't have enough lift, can't quite rise above them. Last night I couldn't fly at all. I was naked, couldn't fly, and had to walk, naked, to a flea market to buy a robe.

Before I go to bed, I watch television with my father. I make sure I'm completely prone on the hospital bed, so he can't accuse me of sitting on it. He has the TV set to the style channel and there's a segment on feng shui. With Seth gone, I am curious how I can move my furniture around to create flowing energy. Maybe I'll get more energy. Maybe I can repair my marriage. Maybe I'll find out if I *want* to repair my marriage.

But this show is not your by-the-book feng shui. It's more feng shui with the rich and famous. A middle-aged woman, a real estate agent who lived in Hong Kong for thirteen years, shows us how she has incorporated feng shui into her California home. A voiceover narrator implies that while in Hong Kong she worked with a feng shui master. What is obvious is she did a lot of shopping. The camera's quick pan of her lavish home shows many bought touches from Asia. Outside you see a mountain range which simulates, the real estate woman tells us, a tortoise. The tortoise theme is carried through to the statuary in her garden—huge sculptures of tortoises, some with wells in their backs to hold water.

"You see a tortoise in the mountain?" my father says hoarsely.

"No," I say, happy to agree.

"What I see is a rich woman who can name her price."

He clears his throat, and I'm not sure he can hear me when I say, "Right."

Though he is talking, I can't believe he is talking. He looks too old to talk or even breathe. He has a beige blanket wrapped around his neck, and the rest of him looks gray and white. It looks to me like he's evaporating, dissipating into the den, later to fall into the back yard as rain. "I think she's Jewish," he says. "With a big ass."

The camera goes into her white bedroom. "White is bad," says the voiceover narrator. "It can promote evil energy. But in the hands of a feng shui master, white can work." The real estate agent stands in front of her four-poster king-size bed, piled high with layers of white linens and white embroidered spreads. It's a wedding cake of a bed, fit for a fat king. The real estate agent holds what looks like a torn red rag in her hand. "I place this," she says, "in between the box spring and the mattress and it wards off evil."

"She gets everything she wants," I say.

"Switch the channel," he says.

"In a minute." I watch as the camera gets close to photos on her bureau.

"Surround yourself," the agent says, "with photos of loved ones. This is a love boudoir. I have no photos of dogs or cats."

"In my bedroom," I say, "I have photos of Rags."

"Better get those out."

We are for now both content and happy with our mutual loathing for the rich feng shui lady. I switch the channel, and Gary Cooper and Grace Kelly are having a dark argument in which I'm shocked to hear Gary say to her, "If you think I like this, you're crazy." She tells him she is leaving on the noon train. I put myself in her shoes, and I think, too bad there isn't an earlier train.

"High noon," I say.

"Leave it," he says. "I don't care."

I say goodnight, offer to help him with anything. I don't think he wears pajamas anymore. Because his days and nights are the same, his day and night clothes are the same. Always now the jog suit. When he was in the nursing home, my mother had his five pieces dry-cleaned and he hasn't asked for them.

"No help necessary," he says, but slurs his words, and I ask him to repeat himself. "Mother will help. You're visiting."

He thinks I'm here for a visit and as I make up the couch in the living room, I imagine I'm a guest, I'm here for a rest, to once again be taken care of. That night, with Rags sleeping on my chest, I lie awake on the sectional and listen for my father falling or dying. He doesn't fall or die, but he does lie on the hospital bed in the den, coughing and listening to Larry King, it seems, all night long. Late into the night, before I finally nod off, I conjure an image of a tortoise at the base of the hospital bed watching over my father, taking over my shift, so I can go to sleep.

In the morning, my mother cooks and prepares his oatmeal and toast as though it's a medical procedure. The heat in the house is up to eighty degrees and I'm wearing gym shorts, a short-sleeve tee, and heavy socks. In this house, you can never be barefoot, because my father has a foot thing. A bare foot has always triggered for him anxiety and rage. To him, a bare foot is a poison pear laced with fungus.

When he has to go to the bathroom, I tie a belt around his waist and hold onto the strap while he leads me with his walker. He walks over the cork floor of the den, each step a shuffle and an effort. He is the pony and I am the cart and the driver. I let the pony enter the bathroom on his own, then I wait outside the door for the sound of a boom or cry. Long before he was a pony, he was wild. He'd rear up and swoop down, spew fire. "Don't sit on the beds!" he'd roar, which we barely heard over his pounding hooves on the hard, cork floor.

After lunch, Rags and I go see Stuart at the store. Upstairs he is with a single customer talking about the history of worsted wool. "Wool was good, but it could feel like tiny pins going into your knees, and some kids, like my sister, had raw thighs from those wool skirts. Now you have the heavy poly-cotton with the same good wear. Only now you got the comfort."

"Huh," the woman says thoughtfully.

Stuart sees Rags and me and says, "Rags. El." Then goes back to his customer. She looks familiar. But I can't remember her name. I forgot lots of names when I left Naugatuck. Five minutes later he's done and walks over to me, where I stand near the BVD display.

"Seth called me last night," he says. "He wanted to know how you were."

"He didn't call me."

"He was probably afraid you'd blow him out of the water." I think Stuart means this as a compliment to me, but I'm not sure. Am I meaner than most people? More angry?

"He didn't say much except the girls missed you. I think he misses you, too."

"Yeah, but when he's with me, he doesn't miss me."

"You giving him a chance?"

"To do, what? Find fault with me? Yes, apparently I'm giving him many chances to do that."

Stuart leans back against the counter with the leather wallets and fleece gloves. "I feel bad for you guys."

Stuart himself is childless and divorced, but in Naugatuck still finds enough women to date, enough sports teams to exercise his identity.

"He seems angry at me all the time," I say.

"Men," Stuart says.

"Men," I say. I stand there looking at Stuart, at his lowered head, his sympathy, and I want to cry. You live and die, you wash dishes, have kids, put thousands of miles on your car, belong to discount buying clubs. Your husband thinks you've fallen short and you thought he was short when you married him. But he was nice then. And your poor brother. He is alone because he's a flawed man and you're alone because you can't live with one. "Gotta go," I say. Stuart knows I'm choked up, and lets me leave. I start down the stairs but when I'm close to the landing, he calls out to me.

"You interviewing help today?"

"Yes," I say, barely able to talk.

"Good luck."

Downstairs, the baby clothes look a bit brighter with the sun out today and blasting through the storefront windows. I'm reminded that thirty years ago, when my mother worked here, she hung infant dresses in the long, silky plastic from the wholesaler. A row of baby dresses, draped with their floor-length plastic capes, looked like tiny bridal superheroes.

I get back in my car, and Rags relinquishes her seat behind the wheel and goes to the passenger side. She looks out the window, happy to see anything. I sit in the car for a few minutes trying not to cry, to think of reasons not to cry. When I was young my father seemed to like me best when we worked at the store together—when there were customers observing us being father and daughter. He'd call me his *asthma baby*, his highest compliment, even though I never had asthma. I had the bad posture; Stuart had the asthma, but he outgrew it. "She's my asthma baby!" he'd say to the long line of rubber workers waiting at the cash register. And to answer their puzzled looks, he'd sing: "*Yes sir, that's my baby / No sir, I don't mean maybe / Yes sir, 'ats ma baby, now.*" Is it wrong to have wished, as I sometimes did, to be asthmatic?

I go back home and when I walk in the front door, my mother says, "Mark Manuscz is here. He's in the den with Dad."

It sounds like she's saying, Mark Manuscz is dead with Dad. I wish I were dead. I look like hell, my hair is frizzy and gray, and I want Mark to think I've done well, that I'm happy with my chosen inseam, with what I have.

She offers Rags a biscuit from her hand and Rags accepts it gently.

They are like two queen mothers, gently extending their gloved hands to each other—reaching toward each other but because of propriety, barely touching. "Mark knows you're here? That's right, you called him about getting a Polish woman. I didn't tell him about Seth and you. I'm sure he'd be very interested."

I can tell my mother is interested too, having a long-time family friend, a podiatrist, still pining for me. She has always liked Seth but, just like laughing at bad news, Dr. and Mrs. Mark Manuscz has a forbidden thrill. "The first Polish woman is coming at eleven. I hope Mark is gone by then; he'll want to run the show." She nods toward the den. "He's trying to push orthotics on Dad, but Dad," she whispers, "is yelling about the money. Go on in."

Rags is searching my mother's open hand for another biscuit, in that way dogs have of thinking magic and good fortune happen to them, to serve their purposes. "All gone, Rags," I say. "Come on." The den door is open and we walk in.

"Ellen," Mark calls out and comes over to kiss my cheek. "Rags," he says, bending down and petting Rags hard behind the ears. I don't think that's Rags' favorite place, but everyone seems to think that's her favorite place. People are always trying to figure out the pleasure points of dogs. Mine is the top of my head, the back of my hand, but no one thinks to look there.

"I'm trying to tell your dad he walks on his heels and an orthotic insert would balance him. He'd be steadier on his feet."

"Your orthotics are a bunch of crap," my father says. "Stuart had two of your orthotics and they made him worse."

"Stuart has bad stenosis."

"You gave him worse stenosis." My father's voice, while weak and raspy, is spirited. His anger, as always, is causing new buds to spawn. He's a study in nature. "You gave Stuart things he didn't have before. Look, you want to visit, visit. You want to say hi to Ellen, say hi to Ellen. But leave my goddamn feet out of it." He is in full bloom.

"So how are you, Ellen?" Mark asks.

"Okay. Trying to get my father what he needs."

"You want to help me?" my father says. "The two of you? My big toe is sore. Can you help that?"

"Let's see," Mark says.

"Oh, sure, you'll look and say, 'orthotic.' Three hundred dollars for a sore toe."

"Shut up and stop being a big fart. Show me your toe."

My father almost smiles. He likes that no-nonsense talk, but if I talked like that he'd kill me.

"It's circulation, Irv. Part of your condition. You need to put your feet up. Your ankles are swollen, too."

"Good. Good-bye. Nice seeing you, Mark. Take Ellen and go."

Mark is happy to take my arm and we walk out of the den. "So how are you?" he asks again.

"Okay." The crook of my arm, I'm thinking, is another pleasure point. And I'm thinking, Mark looking at me is another pleasure point. His face is dark. Dark eyes, dark eyebrows, a smooth, high forehead. Seth looks a lot like him. But Seth's high forehead is usually scowling at me. His curly hair is diminishing, but from time to time a stray curl pokes out from the receding pack and winks at me. His hair remains playful even though he, most of the time, is not. For this reason—not for looks or youth—I want Seth to keep the hair he has.

It is a short walk from the den, down the den steps, through the small narrow hallway, to the kitchen. We pause outside the kitchen door, where two steps away my mother is sitting on her kitchen chair listening to everything. "How's Seth?" Mark asks.

"We're separated. But who knows. Maybe with some rest and separation we can reconnect."

"That's what I said about Mary Ann. Maybe it will work for you."

"Ellen!" my mother calls loudly, knowing I am two steps away from her. "The Polish woman will be here any minute and I need you to do some things for me."

Mark and I pause, look briefly at each other, then walk in the kitchen.

"Hi, Mark," she says. "I'd love to offer you coffee and a piece of Entenmann's but the Polish woman will be here soon and I need to make more notes and talk to Ellen."

"Good luck. If Yvonna comes with her, tell her I said hi, and I'll call her soon. And remember, you can negotiate price a little."

"Thanks," my mother says. "You know, I need to come see you soon. The big toe again. The nail is pressing in. And I like the pens you give out."

"I only give out to you, Mag," he says, giving my arm a squeeze. He kisses her good-bye, he kisses me good-bye, and he's gone.

The doorbell rings and it's Yvonna, the owner of the Polish Place, and the woman Yvonna wants us to interview, Diva. Yvonna looks a little like Ivana Trump and a little like Leona Helmsley. Diva has a face like Meg Ryan and a torso like Madeleine Albright. We all sit around the kitchen table. Before us, against the wall, is the wallpaper mural we've had for fifty years. We should have an anniversary for this mural. It's a Paris street scene with vendors, organ grinder, and monkey. My mother has always said the mural represents the Schmurr family, and, for the benefit of Yvonna and Diva, she points out our Parisian counterparts: a man and woman sitting at a bistro table, a boy running with a loaf of bread, a girl with a balloon. And there we are.

"*Diva*," my mother says. "Like Dee-va?"

"Like Dee-va."

My mother gives a verbal overview of our house. "It's a big house and yet it's not a big house, if you know what I mean, Diva. It seems big but when you think about it, it's just the kitchen, the dining room, the living room, the master bedroom, my little room off the kitchen, and his den, where he spends just about all his time—you know, his TV, his papers everywhere, his phone, he calls his stockbroker." Diva looks at my mother and then looks at Yvonna and says, "Yes? House broken?"

My mother goes on. "Okay, maybe the house *is* big, but we won't ask you to do any major housecleaning. Just him. Just Irv. You take care of Irv. Irv ring bell, you come."

Diva looks at my mother and I get the feeling she would like to put her fingers in my mother's mouth to get a handle on what the hell my mother is saying. "Yes? Irv, bell?"

Yvonna and Diva leave, and a half hour later Yvonna's associate, Tina, and another applicant, Marguerite, come. Tina looks like Ivana Trump at seventy-two with a long, blond ponytail. "I Yvonna's helper. Anything you want tell Yvonna you tell me. Is okay." Marguerite, the applicant, looks like a strapping Margaux Hemingway and I wonder why she wants to live here, bathe, feed, and change my father's wet clothes. Tina introduces Marguerite by saying she's learning English and she likes to paint on big canvases.

My mother nods, as though this is exactly what she has asked for. She starts in again.

"Marguerite, it may seem like a big house and it is maybe a big house but your job will be Irv. You take care of Irv. Period. He needs help walking, you help him walk. He needs help going to bathroom, you help him go. Getting dressed? You dress. Have you done that before?"

"Yes?" Marguerite pauses and continues to look at my mother as if looking for clues.

"He has congestive heart failure," my mother goes on, "and he's weak and he doesn't sleep. He, Irv. Weak. So you may need to catch some rest during the day, if you're with him at night. Do you drive?"

"Yes? I can?"

"Say, if we needed you to go to the CVS for medication, could you drive?"

"Yes?"

"You have license?"

"I think it's okay." She looks over to Tina and then down at her own lap and swallows. I can hear her swallow.

My mother cups a hand over her mouth and says, "Tina, I think we're having a communication problem. Tina, you hear me?" Marguerite stares at my mother. We're all staring at my mother. "I don't think we're understanding each other."

"She's learning," Tina says. "In Poland, she's engineer."

My mother sighs and goes on. "Marguerite, if you want to paint, we set up canvas and easel in your room and you can paint. What you like to paint? You paint trees? A man?"

"I paint. Here, there. I big colors."

"You color hair?" my mother asks her and points to her own hair. "The roots. I see you have roots. You color hair?"

"Mom!" I say, and I clutch Marguerite's forearm.

"Is okay," Marguerite says, patting my arm.

My mother doggedly presses on, putting her fingertips into the scalp of her own hair. "I've colored my hair for fifty years. I still use the same shade I used back then. I mix Autumn Maple Glade with Harvest Ember. Maybe Harvest Umber."

"No, I . . . No," she says to my mother.

Rags is under the table, at my feet, and I pat her, let her lick my fingers. By mistake I stick a finger in her eye, but she doesn't care. She's forgiving and interprets all touch as love, unless I hit her hard under the chin.

"Okay," my mother says. "Just woman talk." To Tina, she says, "I just don't know, Tina."

"We try again with someone else," Tina says. "What you want?"

"Fluent isn't necessary, but she should at least understand me and speak fairly well."

"They get more."

"Like, for example?"

"One hundred fifty dollars per day."

"We're on a limited income."

"Everyone limited. But okay. I bring you tomorrow." They leave quickly by the back door next to the washing machine.

I give Tina a handshake, then return to the kitchen table. "I can't believe you asked about her hair."

"What? I thought it broke the ice. But I don't know. One loser after another. Let's see what Yvonna can bring tomorrow."

My mother and I make dinner and I serve my father in the den. "I hate chicken," he says. "Everything with her is chicken. She's trying to kill me with chicken. I had chicken last night."

"That was scrod."

"Well, it tasted like chicken. Tell her I want fish tomorrow." I don't say anything but leave the den and start doing dishes. The doorbell rings.

"Oh, it could be Brandon," my mother says. "I owe him for shoveling us out—the last snow."

It's Seth. And the girls.

"Ellen," my mother calls out. Go down to the basement refrigerator and bring up an Entenmann's."

Jill comes in the door, gives me a hug, and says, "Na, na," which is her babyish, affectionate form of Mama. Paula says, "We miss you."

Seth says, "How's your father?" He's scowling as he walks through the washing machine alcove. He looks like a shadow attached to a rigid, steel outline of a man. "Girls, come on," he says, leading the way into the den.

"What does Dad know?" I ask my mother, who is sitting on her chair. "About Seth and me."

"Nothing."

"Stuart and I think it best that Dad doesn't know about us. That Seth has his own apartment."

"I hope the girls don't say anything to Dad," my mother says.

"They're afraid to say anything to him."

"Then I think you're safe."

The girls come out of the den in two minutes, then go into the living room to watch TV.

I follow them into the living room. "You give Grandpa a hug?"

"Kinda," they say, looking at the TV, not me. My mother lets them eat their Entenmann's in front of the TV in the living room. I never let them eat outside the kitchen; I learned that from my father. The girls know they'll see me tomorrow evening so they don't need to be with me now. Instead, they apparently need to watch *The Simpsons*, where they can take comfort in Homer's latest fall from grace. It must reassure them that someone so stupid manages to stay alive, episode to episode.

Seth is still in the den with my father when the doorbell rings. I look through the venetian blinds in my old room and see a car I don't recognize. Still, I have a feeling, and when I open the door Mark is standing on the porch steps. He is wearing a navy down jacket that falls high on the hip. I walk out on the porch to see him. It must be thirty-five degrees but I don't put on a jacket; I won't be out long.

"I came to say, go and have a good life. Try to mend things with Seth."

"Really?" I say.

"No, not really." And then we are kissing. I'm not sure I'm kissing him but he's kissing me. Now he's hugging me and while I'm not hugging back I'm standing there allowing myself to be warmed. His arms are buried beneath the sleeves of his puffy jacket, but I know his arms are under there, just as I know the inseam is still there. This isn't love; this is a tiny inlet where I can pull over and rest my oars.

Finally, I pull away. "It's cold and Seth's inside," I say.

"Jesus! Seth's inside? I'm out of here. I don't want to get us shot. I'm really trying to do the right thing. I'm gone. I've left."

"Go. That would be the right thing."

He gives me one last kiss. A soft, slow one and he's gone, without another word, because, I think, he doesn't have any words to say. Even "bye" would be wrong.

I go back in, and as the warmth of the house hits my face I'm suddenly freezing. I open the coat closet, put on my red ski parka, and go in the kitchen, where my mother is sitting in her chair.

"Who was that?" she asks, then mouths the word, "Mark?"

"Yes."

"Don't ask for trouble," she whispers.

I open the refrigerator to get some Coke or cold chicken or anything to change my dreamy mood. Mark's smell is still in my nose. He had the smell twenty years ago. These days Seth is odorless; I can't smell him anymore. He keeps it to himself.

While I'm rummaging behind the refrigerator door, poking a finger into a tiny dish of leftover egg salad, I hear Seth come into the kitchen. I kneel down low and open the fruit drawer. I just don't want to see him right now.

"Okay, quick visit," he says. "The girls have school tomorrow. Where's Ellen?"

"Right here," my mother says.

"Right here," I say coming up with an apple.

"Why do you have on your parka?"

"I was going to take Rags for a walk."

"I'll come, too."

So we get Rags and start off. "Your father seems okay," Seth says. "I mean he looks tired and old. He has no strength. But he said to me, 'Nice to see you, Seth,' and I think he meant it."

"He always liked you."

"What's not to like?"

I don't answer.

"What's not to like?"

"You always seem mad."

"Because *you* always seem mad. You always seem to have a bad word for me. *I'm a slob. I eat too fast. I mumble.* I feel you don't appreciate me."

"I feel you don't appreciate me, either."

"I said it first."

"I do appreciate you, Seth. I do."

"Can we try to be nicer to each other?" he asks. "Can we just make the effort?"

"Can *you* try?"

"Can *you* try?"

"Yes," I say. I'll try. I really don't want to try, but at the moment I smell wood smoke, a smell that always makes me hopeful. So I dig deep to find something about Seth that makes me hopeful and I think, the smell of his scalp. It used to have an earth smell: earth, oil, soil.

"Can I smell your head?" I ask, and he lets me. He takes off his knit cap and lets me. And there we are, Rags by my side, and I'm all nose, trying to bring back an old scent. What I come up with, however, is more cold air and the strong smell of wood burning.

That night, after everyone is gone, I put on my pajamas and robe and go into the den to watch TV with my father. "You like that hospital bed?" my father asks me.

"Yes."

"I hate it."

Apparently my father is still watching the feng shui channel, for here we are again. We're seeing the home of a Dr. Fishkind and the doctor is wearing a navy blazer and an ascot.

"Dad, he's wearing an ascot. I didn't think men wore ascots anymore."

"He's a jerk. With too much money."

My father dozes on and off—he floats in and out; I'm not sure what he sees and doesn't see. If he even registers that the TV is on. The Dr. Fishkind segment includes scenes with the doctor's grown son, a thirty-year-old man, who is showing the feng shui in Dr. Fishkind's bathroom. The old son sits, fully clothed, in an empty, dry Jacuzzi. "This is a gold and marble inlay Jacuzzi," he says, the camera catching all the candles lining the shelves of the marble backsplash. "It's my favorite place," the son says, "when my mom's away on business."

I am repulsed by the psychology here: a thirty-year-old son, waiting for his mother to leave so he can light her candles and soak naked in her Jacuzzi. I look over at my father, who seems to be watching, but I'm not sure he's taking it in. Still, I play the daughter asking her father questions: "Doesn't the son have a job?" I ask. "Why's an old son in his mother's bathtub?"

"You've done well," he says. "Not everybody does so well. You've got your own tub."

"I've done okay," I say. But I pretend to be modest so I can take in what he's said to me: *You've got your own tub.* He has actually paid me a compliment. He's paid me. My father, who thinks he's got nothing, has paid me. You've got your own tub. And I do. I have a tub, a house, a family. Rather, I might have a tub. Right now, I don't know what I have.

He's getting sleepy again. "Turn the channel," he says. I turn it to some old movie in which I recognize no one. He closes his eyes, folds his hands in his lap, and says, "Leave it there," so I leave the channel just where it is and we say goodnight.

That night I listen for him falling and he does fall. I hear a crash and go into the den and there he is on the floor near the TV. "I was trying to get to the bathroom by myself," he says, "and I didn't make it." I try to lift him up, which is stupid. I'm tired and go for the dead lift. I put my arms under his and just pull with all my might. This gets me nowhere except on the floor with him. Suddenly we're eye to eye. "You're good for nothing," he says to me.

"So are you," I say to him.

He starts laughing and I start laughing. We are on the cork floor, side by side, looking into each other's eyes and laughing.

The next day, first thing, nine o'clock, Yvonna shows up with another applicant, Vivka. "She just came off another job," Yvonna says, "but the man not need her," which I take to mean, the man died.

Vivka looks about fifty, but fifty long years in Poland.

"She speak well and she take care of men. She good."

We sit at the kitchen table.

"Vivka, what's your experience taking care of people?" my mother begins.

"I take care of doctor's father for a long time and doctor here write me letter of introduction."

My mother holds the heavy piece of writing paper and we both read the doctor's letter. Vivka took good care of his father. She was strong, caring, uncomplaining, and diligent. She drove, she cooked, she treated him like a king. "The doctor's father was a big man," she says, "and I do everything for him. I wash him and dress him and help him walk. I change diaper. I also cook, clean, whatever you want me to do, I do."

She doesn't look at Yvonna, she looks at my mother. "You heve nice house. I don't need much space. You heve bed for me here, I fine. I heve my own apartment in New Britain, which I keep, where my mail come and if I can go home once a week, once every two week, I fine with you." She pats her left breast to show everything is fine with her if everything is fine with us. It is. She wants to be paid under the table; we are fine with this. She wants to go home once a week. Fine. She will start right away. She has food and clothes in New Britain. She'll get her clothes and be back in two hours, bring to my parents the pierogis and cake she has already made, not expecting she would be taking a job today.

"Irv might eat a nice pierogi," my mother says, which we all take to mean the deal is sealed.

We take Vivka to the den to meet my father. I stand in the doorway of the den with Rags at my feet. My mother takes Vivka halfway into the room and the two of them stand before him. He's sitting in the rocking chair watching TV with the volume up high.

"Turn off the TV," my mother says. Emeril is cooking a veal stew.

"Go away," he says. "I didn't ask for anybody."

"I want you to meet Vivka. We want to hire her for you. Turn off the TV."

He picks up the remote, makes a big deal of looking down at it and pressing a button.

"Nice to meet you," he says, his face still looking down at the remote. "Now leave me alone, if you don't mind. I don't feel well." No one budges and he looks up. "You look like a nice woman. But no thank you to your help. I've got something else in mind." To my mother he says, "Leave it to you. She's got a tuchus as big as a train."

"He doesn't know what he's saying half the time," my mother says to Vivka.

"She doesn't know what I'm saying but I know what I'm saying and what I'm saying is she has a big, fat . . ."

"Dad, cut the crap," I say loudly from the doorway. "We have a nice woman here." Rags starts barking just then. She goes into the middle of the room, looks at me, and starts barking. "It's all right, Rags," I say. She goes over to me and barks and then goes to my father and barks. "If your plan is to work Mom into the grave with your demands and insults, I won't allow it."

"The dog's upset," my father says, with disgust and weariness.

"You're a pain in the ass," I say, walking into the middle of the room and patting Rag's head. "Dad, it's either Vivka or Harbor View. Since your insurance ran out, Harbor View is two hundred sixty dollars a day. Vivka is one hundred dollars. And you get to stay in your home. I have to get back to New London. What's it going to be?"

"Vivka. Vivka? Her name is Vivka?"

Vivka says, "Viv-ka or Viv-ki."

"I'll call her Vicki."

"It's all right," she says. "You cull me anything."

"Vicki, then."

"Okay," she says, and the deal is sealed.

In the hall, walking toward the kitchen, my mother says, "Vivka, this is what he's like. You've seen it. Can you handle it?"

"None worry. I take care of him. He not feel good."

"Thank you," I say, holding her arm. "Thank you."

I pack my things, then go to say good-bye to him. I'm scared to death to face him, to open the den door. But I have no choice.

He's sitting in his rocker, but he has a ledger on his lap, where he is recording numbers. "I'm cold," he says when I walk in. "Bring me my heavy suit jacket. It's in the hall closet."

I rummage through the closet.

"It's still in the plastic from the cleaner. Mother cleaned it on me, when I was in Harbor View." He starts coughing and because of the throat singers, I recognize the sound. It begins as the sound of a wineglass being clinked, then changes to the growling of a wolf. I find the coat and bring it to him. I have to put his hand in the sleeve and then he can manage to push the arm through. "I'm always cold," he says.

"I know," I say. "I'm sorry. You want some coffee and Entenmann's?"
He shakes his head. "I have a big mouth. I know it."

I don't say anything, my terror resumed. I was lucky once, but I won't test it again.

"I know you and Seth are separated. He told me. Why didn't you tell me?"

"I was scared."

"Look. You work it out. Whatever it takes, you work it out. You got two kids. Look at Mother and me. We stay together for you." He starts to laugh but is interrupted by some coughing. "A parent will always be a parent. Your kids will always need you."

"I know," I say, and start to cry.

"Don't cry. Go and do as I say. I told Seth the same thing. So, go and set things right. Next time I see you, I want it straightened out." He takes a roll of bills from his pocket, the ancestral father's money roll. It's part of his uniform, like the stained jacket, like the vest. He peels off some tens, some twenties. "Buy something that looks nice. You look like hell. And one more thing."

I'm sure he's going to say the thing I can carry with me, the good word.

"Next time I see you . . ."

He coughs a cough, a low guttural sound which simulates the battering of horse hooves. I wait.

". . . I want you to be a blond."

I stop to see Stuart at the store on my way out of town. It's cold and overcast, though the clouds look like there's some light behind them, like an X-ray film on the doctor's light board. I bring Rags into Schmurr's to say good-bye to Stuart. It's four o'clock and he has some customers who have stopped by after their shift at Risdon, after picking up their kids from basketball practice. He's with a teenage boy talking about running.

"Your problem is, you run on your toes. And your stride is hard. You should think about having an easy stride, easy stride. El. Rags."

"I don't want to interrupt you but we hired a woman. She seems good, she speaks English, and I told off Dad. Now I have to get back."

"No, no wait. We're finished here." He turns to the boy and extends his hand for a handshake. "Ray, good man. It's just some mechanical things you need to work out."

If the day comes when the Catholics stop wearing school uniforms, Stuart could hold formal running workshops at the Marriot, and his old customers would pay to attend. He's that good.

"You hired someone and told off Dad?"

"I did it all."

"I'd never have the nerve to tell him off. You're my hero."

"Likewise." I blush and I can feel it—the rush of blood to my cheeks. "And the woman seems good. If you go over there in an hour, you can check her out and have some pierogis. She's keeping her apartment, and probably wants a day off here and there, but otherwise she's game to live in."

"She going to stay tonight?"

"Yep."

"Good work, El. My little sister. I'll walk you to your car." He calls out to the few customers. "I'll be back in a minute."

We walk out to the Caprice, parked in front on Maple Street. "How many miles on this?"

"One hundred fifty thousand. Seth wants to get up to two hundred."

"You gonna let him?"

"Maybe."

"Men are tough," he says.

I look at him and he doesn't seem tough. He is a likeness of me, with less gray, even though he is older. His skin is fair, his eyes are fair—a little Danny Kaye around the eyes and brow, a little Bono in the nose, a little Madonna around the mouth. And so am I. We could be in movies or on stage but instead we are here.

I lean against my Caprice and wrap my worn, red parka around me. It's cold, but Stuart is just wearing a sweater with big geometric designs on it. And his running shoes. Always his running shoes. If he thinks of running this store as an athletic event, he can keep it going—it's an act of imagination that keeps the store afloat.

I look at the storefront window, packed with clothes, silver tinsel, fake presents wrapped in red. He's got big paper snowflakes floating among the sweatshirts and the Lee jeans, the navy slacks, the box-pleat skirts. I'm remembering that twenty-four years ago at Christmas time, my father wore Christmas ties and put on a good mood for the customers. He massaged the big bull necks of the rubber workers as they clustered around the cash register. He'd call out, "Deck those halls with matzo balls!"

"El," he'd say, to get my attention, as I stood before the cash register, ringing up sales in my own wool skirt, not a uniform, but a kilt. I'm remembering his Christmas cheer. "Ellen," he'd say, again, and I knew he was pulling me into his cheerleader routine. "Matzo, Matzo!" he'd call out.

"Balls, Balls, Balls," I said. It was my line. It always got a laugh.

"That's my baby," he announced to the customers. "At's my baby. Asthma baby." Then he'd sing, loudly: "Yessir, asthma baby. No sir, I don't mean maybe. Yes sir, asthma baby, now."

It was our song.

ACKNOWLEDGMENTS

THANK YOU to Tom Drury for appreciating my work and selecting my collection for the Iowa Short Fiction Award.

And tremendous thanks to those who have been my lifeline:

Steve Machuga, my husband and champion, who helped me buy my first computer, drove me out to Iowa thirty plus years ago, and has been my best friend for a long time.

Caroline Rosenstone, who spontaneously quotes from my stories and, during my New Haven years, fed and inspired me.

My Writers' Group: Wally Lamb, Bruce Cohen, Leslie Johnson, Denise Abercrombie, Jon Anderson, and Doug Hood. My other dear writer friends: Elizabeth Bobrick, Rachel Basch, Deborah Cannarella, Terri Klein, Indira Ganesan, Suzanne Berne, Eileen Pollack, Jenny Lecce, Alice Mattison, Robb-Forman Dew, and the late James Allen McPherson, who encouraged my work and taught me how to vacuum my rug.

My long-time ardent supporters: Katherine Clay, Mary Dean, Jayne Fishkind, Denise and Scott Levy, Alan Franzi, Susan and Julie Rosenblatt, and the Machuga family—all of them.

Students, faculty, and staff at the Educational Center for the Arts in New Haven, Connecticut.

And my big brothers, Howard and Steve Rosenblatt, who shepherded me through my childhood and still always make me laugh.

"Miss McCook" and "Harvester" were originally published in the *Iowa Review*. "Sweethearts" and "As in Life" were both published in *Glimmer Train*. "The New Frontier" and "Communion" were both published in *Nimrod International Journal of Prose and Poetry*.

THE IOWA SHORT FICTION AWARD AND THE
JOHN SIMMONS SHORT FICTION AWARD WINNERS,
1970–2020

James Fetler
Impossible Appetites
Starkey Flythe Jr.
Lent: The Slow Fast
Kathleen Founds
*When Mystical Creatures
Attack!*
Sohrab Homi Fracis
*Ticket to Minto: Stories of
India and America*
H. E. Francis
The Itinerary of Beggars
Abby Frucht
Fruit of the Month
Tereze Glück
*May You Live in Interesting
Times*
Ivy Goodman
Heart Failure
Barbara Hamby
Lester Higata's 20th Century
Edward Hamlin
*Night in Erg Chebbi and
Other Stories*
Ann Harleman
Happiness
Elizabeth Harris
The Ant Generator
Ryan Harty
*Bring Me Your Saddest
Arizona*
Charles Haverty
Excommunicados

Mary Hedin
Fly Away Home
Beth Helms
American Wives
Jim Henry
*Thank You for Being
Concerned and Sensitive*
Allegra Hyde
Of This New World
Matthew Lansburgh
Outside Is the Ocean
Lisa Lenzo
Within the Lighted City
Kathryn Ma
*All That Work and Still
No Boys*
Renée Manfredi
Where Love Leaves Us
Susan Onthank Mates
The Good Doctor
John McNally
Troublemakers
Molly McNett
One Dog Happy
Tessa Mellas
Lungs Full of Noise
Kate Milliken
*If I'd Known You Were
Coming*
Kevin Moffett
Permanent Visitors
Lee B. Montgomery
Whose World Is This?

Anthony Varallo
This Day in History
Ruvanee Pietersz Vilhauer
*The Water Diviner and
Other Stories*
Don Waters
Desert Gothic
Lex Williford
Macauley's Thumb
Miles Wilson
Line of Fall

Russell Working
Resurrectionists
Emily Wortman-Wunder
Not a Thing to Comfort You
Ashley Wurzbacher
Happy Like This
Charles Wyatt
Listening to Mozart
Don Zancanella
Western Electric